"Why can't you take no for an answer?"

Ken asked her.

The atmosphere around them seemed charged. So much adrenaline was surging through Randy that her knees shook. "I've told you that I call the shots as I see them."

Ken's powerful form actually quivered as he fought for control. "I know exactly what kind of biased article you'd write," he said.

Randy glared at him, her green eyes like ice. "Take your hands off me!"

Ken realized to his horror that he had grabbed Randy's wrist. He dropped it hastily, but not before the warm silkiness of her skin made its impact. He could feel that warmth, that silkiness curl like perfumed smoke through his veins.

Locking his hands behind his back, he growled, "Why can't you just go home?"

Once more their eyes clashed like drawn blades, and this time Randy's knees held firm. "No way, mister," she told him. "Not until I've done what I came here to do."

Dear Reader,

Aahh...the lazy days of August. Relax in your favorite lawn chair with a glass of ice-cold lemonade and the perfect summertime reading...Silhouette Romance novels.

Silhouette Romance books *always* reflect the magic of love in compelling stories that will make you laugh and cry and move you time and time again. This month is no exception. Our heroines find happiness with the heroes of their dreams—from the boy next door to the handsome, mysterious stranger. We guarantee their heartwarming stories of love will delight you.

August continues our WRITTEN IN THE STARS series. Each month in 1991, we're proud to present a book that focuses on the hero—and his astrological sign. This month, we feature the proud, charismatic and utterly charming Leo man in Kasey Michaels's *Lion on the Prowl*.

In the months to come, watch for Silhouette Romance books by your all-time favorites, including Diana Palmer, Brittany Young and Annette Broadrick. We're pleased to bring you books with Silhouette's distinctive blend of charm, wit and—above all—romance. Your response to these stories is a touchstone for us. We'd love to hear from you!

Sincerely,

Valerie Susan Hayward
Senior Editor

SHARON FRANCIS

Irresistible Force

Silhouette Romance

Published by Silhouette Books New York

America's Publisher of Contemporary Romance

To "The Friday Lunch Group"

SILHOUETTE BOOKS
300 E. 42nd St., New York, N.Y. 10017

IRRESISTIBLE FORCE

ISBN: 0-373-08811-6

First Silhouette Books printing August 1991

Books by Sharon Francis

Silhouette Romance

Hot Time #769
Irresistible Force #811

SHARON FRANCIS

now makes her home with her husband in Massachusetts, where they've raised two grown sons, but her beginnings are far more exotic. Born at the foot of the mountains in Japan, she has also lived in Thailand, and still visits Japan regularly. Sharon was fourteen years old when she was first published—a short story in an English teen magazine—and she has since made her mark both in romance writing and elsewhere, with over thirty published titles to her credit, written under several names.

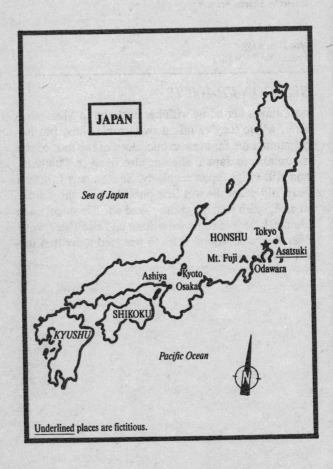

JAPAN

Sea of Japan

HONSHU

Tokyo

Mt. Fuji △ **Asatsuki**

Ashiya **Kyoto** Odawara

Osaka

SHIKOKU

KYUSHU

Pacific Ocean

N

<u>Underlined</u> places are fictitious.

Chapter One

So this was the troublemaker. Randy pushed aside a spray of bamboo and took a good look at Yoshitsune's Rock.

It was incredible that so many people were up in arms over an ordinary-looking chunk of granite, crusted with lichen and surrounded with patches of moss. But then the world was full of astonishing things. No matter how often she flew, Randy couldn't get over the fact that she could cover thirteen thousand miles in little more than half a day. It was hard to believe that right now New York was slumbering peacefully while she was in Japan and standing on Yui Hill.

Randy got down on her knees beside Yoshitsune's Rock. She adjusted the lens of her camera and tried to find an angle that would give it some grandeur. The rock really didn't look like much, yet long ago it had been witness to a moment of love and tragedy. And the moss that surrounded it was *the* moss that was so important to her friend Minny.

"I hope you get your man," a deep voice said behind her.

Randy turned her head and saw someone walking toward her up the slope of the hill. His back was to the light, so her first impression was of breadth of shoulder and height. He had to be at least six feet tall, and in Japan, land of slender, slightly built people, that definitely made him stand out.

He'd also spoken in English. A tourist? Randy wondered.

The stranger continued, "Unmarried girls come up here to ask Yoshitsune's sweetheart to send them husbands."

She couldn't remember reading anything like that in her guidebook. "Is that a local custom?" she asked.

He nodded. "Not many people outside of Asatsuki know about it. Anyway, I doubt if you need Lady Shizuka's help."

Randy wasn't sure whether that was a compliment, an observation or a pass. He'd come close enough for her to see the way the sun caught copper glints in his thick dark hair and found flecks of gold in his tawny eyes. His nose was boldly aquiline, and his square jaw unsoftened by its cleft, but he had a pleasant smile. A man of contrasts, Randy thought, even to his clothes. Though he wore a worker's coveralls and mud-splashed boots, he looked like a man more used to giving orders than taking them.

Perhaps he was a construction foreman? She'd seen work crews clearing the land on her way to the hill. But those work crews were quite some distance away, and besides, they'd all been Japanese. The man before her had European features.

"Did you know that you're on private property?" he was asking.

Perhaps he was part of Sawa Industries's security. "I didn't see any No Trespassing signs," Randy hedged.

"They're all in Japanese."

When he smiled, his eyes warmed until they were almost gold, Randy noted. Aloud she said, "I'm sorry if I've offended anyone. I knew that the hill was going to be a part of Sawa Town, but I didn't think to ask permission before climbing up here."

He looked surprised but pleased. "Are they talking about Sawa Town in Kansas?"

So he'd pegged her accent. His own, with those broad vowels, was harder to place. Boston, perhaps, Randy thought, as she explained, "I come from Meldon, a small town north of Topeka. How did you guess?"

"My roommate at Harvard was from Wichita." He held out his hand, adding, "I'm Kenjiro Sawa. Or Ken, as my American friends call me."

Junjiro's son! Randy frankly stared. Though she had several photos of Ken Sawa's industrialist father, the self-styled "shogun of modern industry" looked nothing like the man before her.

Then she recalled she'd read that Junjiro had been married to a Norwegian aviatrix. The late Nora Helgar must have been Kenjiro's mother. Randy took his proffered hand, saying, "Glad to meet you, Mr. Sawa. I'm Randy Muir."

He'd heard that name somewhere before. Or perhaps the odd sense of recognition was due to the fact that he enjoyed looking at Randy Muir. Her heart-shaped face, framed by a shoulder-length fall of shining dark brown hair, was open and intelligent. Her small nose, which presently supported dark sunglasses, was shapely. Her mouth had a lovely, generous curve.

The rest of her curved, too, in all the right places. Ken noted that her cream-colored slacks showed off her shapely thighs and bottom, and that her green silk blouse under the windbreaker emphasized her feminine form. And she didn't wear the clanking jewelry to which most Western tourists seemed addicted.

A very attractive woman, he thought. "Welcome to Japan," he told her, "and please do call me Ken."

Throughout the years, Randy had developed the theory that handshakes were as distinctive as fingerprints. There were the hearty crushers, the amorous palmers and the businesslike brisks. Ken Sawa's handshake was harder to place. Her hand was lost in his, but its firm pressure was also considerately gentle.

These impressions didn't tally with what she knew about the Sawa family. According to the articles and news clips she'd read, Junjiro liked to refer to his industrial empire as a kingdom and to himself as a benevolent shogun. Shoguns were historically cold-blooded, scheming types, but there was nothing cold about Ken Sawa. In fact, the interested look in his amber eyes was causing her emotional thermostat to nudge several degrees upward.

"I wanted to speak to your father before coming up here," she said aloud. "I tried phoning him this afternoon at the Sawa Building here in Asatsuki, but his secretary told me he was at his family home in Ashiya."

He looked puzzled. "Why would you want to speak to my father?"

"Actually I wanted to request an interview with him. I'm here to do an article for *Issues Today*."

It was surprising how quickly his expression changed. From cordial, appreciative and definitely interested, it went directly to wary. "An article," he repeated.

"Yes. Perhaps you'll recall that I wrote to you some time ago?"

So *that* was why Randy Muir's name had sounded so familiar. "I remember," Ken said.

His voice clipped the words, and he'd let go of her hand. The chill in his voice reduced the early April day to a near-freezing temperature. It didn't take a genius to guess that Ken Sawa was opposed to the idea of an article, Randy thought, and that was really too bad. He'd seemed like an open-minded man, one with whom she'd enjoy doing business.

Now she'd have to explain and negotiate. But before she could do either, he was saying, "An interview with my father is out of the question. He's not well."

"Then perhaps you'd consent to an interview yourself?" When he didn't respond, she added, "Will you at least let me explain the gist of my article? I think you'll find the concept intriguing.''

"Go ahead, I'm listening."

Ken sat down on Yoshitsune's Rock and stretched his long legs. "I'm running on a tight time frame these days," he continued, "but I have a few minutes now. Take a load off your feet, Randy Muir, and tell me what's on your mind."

The idea of using the historical rock as a chair seemed disrespectful somehow. "I'd rather stand," Randy said firmly.

"Afraid of the spirit of Yoshitsune, eh?"

There was a hint of mockery in his voice, and those golden eyes were assessing her keenly. Randy recalled that to the Japanese, "face" was everything. If he felt she didn't dare sit on the Rock of Yoshitsune, she'd lose face with this disconcerting man.

As she lowered herself onto a corner of the rock, he observed, "See? No thunderbolts. No *ninja* warriors leaping out of the shrubbery to attack you. It's just an ordinary rock."

It was also a very small rock. Randy found herself so near to Ken that only a few inches separated them. At such close quarters, she was aware of subtleties—of the way his dark hair grew straight near the crown of his head but had a definite curl at the nape of his neck; of the unexpectedly delicate shape of his ears. Her brother Charlie, also a big man but a pussycat at heart, had ears like that.

Randy reminded herself that Ken Sawa was hardly a pussycat. His golden eyes stayed focused on her with a disturbing steadiness as she marshaled her facts.

"Japan is very much in the news these days," she began. "*Issues Today* is intrigued by the clash between old, traditional ideas and the rapid modernization in this country. We feel that the problem Sawa Industries is having with the Greater Kanto Historical Society is typical of this conflict."

"I hardly think that Sawa Town is typical of anything," Ken interrupted.

"That wasn't what I meant," Randy protested.

When he shifted on the rock, his knee brushed hers. "Then what did you mean?"

"We're talking about a major confrontation here. In order to build its industrial-residential complex, Sawa Industries means to destroy not only Yoshitsune's Rock but Yui Hill itself. Meanwhile the Greater Kanto Historical Society has taken the position that the rock is historically important. The society believes that the shogun Minamoto Yoritomo's younger brother, Yoshitsune, came here to Asatsuki in 1189 A.D., and that he met his faithful sweetheart, Lady Shizuka, on Yui Hill before he went on to Mutsu and his death."

"Their claims aren't substantiated by facts." Ken heard the irritation in his own voice and forced himself to speak more calmly. "You have to understand that Yoshitsune is to Japan what El Cid is to Spain. He was a poet, a warrior and he was only thirty when he died. There are hundreds of legends about him."

"But Yoshitsune did come this way before Yoritomo had him hunted down," Randy argued. "If Lady Shizuka also came to Asatsuki, it's possible they met here."

"Possible but not likely."

Maybe he was concerned about her credentials? "This isn't the first time I've handled a controversial issue," Randy pointed out. "I'm a senior writer for *Issues Today*. Before joining the magazine, I was an investigative reporter for the *Topeka Herald*."

"I'm sure you're very capable."

He sounded polite but unconvinced. She wasn't getting anywhere, so she tried another tack. "This isn't just an assignment for me," Randy said. "I've been intrigued by Japan since I was a little girl. I also have a very good Japanese friend, Minako Watanabe, who was an exchange student when I was in high school. Minny's now an assistant professor of botany at Ohashi University, not far from Tokyo."

"And no doubt you informed your *dear* friend that you were coming to Japan."

When he narrowed his eyes like that, his face took on a distinctly arrogant look. You're here to do a job, Randy reminded herself. Don't blow it.

"Certainly I told Minny I was coming. When I did, she told me about the other controversy surrounding the rock. Apparently Yui Hill is the only place where *Ephemerum hygromatica* grows."

"Apparently your friend neglected to inform you that *Ephemerum hygromatica* is of no use to anyone or anything." Ken scuffed at a bit of moss with the toe of his boot, adding, "You can hardly see it without a magnifying glass."

"To a botanist, its loss would be a tragedy. When I spoke with her last, she and some colleagues from

Ohashi University were going to meet with you to explain their position."

Abruptly he rose to his feet. "Look, I'm familiar with the John Wayne mentality."

"I don't follow you."

"Good guys against bad guys. David versus Goliath. Your article would undoubtedly cast Sawa Industries as a bully."

"And that's far from true, of course."

Try as she would, she couldn't keep a dollop of sarcasm out of her voice. He shot her a dirty look before asking, "Have you ever read Tennyson?"

The rapid change of subject made her blink. "Ah, what?"

"Alfred Lord Tennyson was a nineteenth-century British poet. He said, 'The old order changeth, yielding place to new,/ lest one good custom should corrupt the world.' What happened in the twelfth century doesn't matter anymore."

As he finished speaking, Ken got to his feet. His movement was so swift and unexpected that Randy almost lost her precarious seat on the rock. She was forced to scrabble for balance, an indignity that was compounded when he reached out to steady her.

His grip on her arms was strong and sure. Randy resented both his assurance and strength. Even so, she gave it one last try.

Withdrawing her arm from his grasp, she spoke with as much conviction as she could muster. "If you'd read any one of my previously published articles, you'll see that I don't editorialize. I bend over backward to show every viewpoint. Why not use my article as a forum for your views?"

"Sawa Industries doesn't need a forum."

The man had an attitude problem, and she'd about had it with him. With an effort, Randy reigned in her temper and said peaceably, "I'd like to hear that from Mr. Sawa, Sr., personally. I'll go to Ashiya—"

She wasn't prepared for the blaze in his eyes, and his voice was a muted roar. "You're not to disturb my father in any way. Is that clear?"

"But I wouldn't disturb him—"

"No, because you won't go near him. Why do you think he went to Ashiya? He's too ill to be bothered by a pack of fools."

Clearly he considered her one of the fools. Randy whipped off her glasses and drew herself to her full five foot seven inches in order to glare more effectively at Ken Sawa.

"It's a free country, or at least it was, last thing I heard. I'll go where I want and I'll write as I see fit."

About to snap back an answer, Ken found himself staring into green eyes that reflected both the emerald of Randy's shirt and the softer color of the new leaves budding on Yui Hill. They were remarkable eyes, large, clear and flashing with indignation.

Though they were almost nose to nose, Randy Muir wasn't backing down. She wasn't one to take "no" for an answer, and that could cause problems. In other circumstances, Ken might have admired her feisty spirit, but right now he was in no mood to do so. This pigheaded, green-eyed woman had no idea how high the stakes were or what her obstinacy was putting at risk.

"I can't stop you from staying in Asatsuki," he gritted, "but I can and will make sure that you don't trespass on our property or bother our workers."

Randy tried for a steadying breath and drew in a lungful of air tinged with Ken Sawa's cologne. It was totally illogical that even while she was so mad at him she could have spit in his eye, she was very much aware of that clean, virile scent.

"I won't need to," she retorted. "I'm sure the people of Asatsuki will be happy to tell me how they feel about Sawa Town and the destruction of their hill."

Without waiting for his reaction, Randy turned on her heel and began to walk past him down the mountain path. How could she have thought, even for a moment, that Ken Sawa was a reasonable man? He was egocentric, stubborn, insensitive and controlling.

She was so angry that she didn't see the root that snaked over the narrow path. She stumbled and might have fallen if he hadn't reached out and caught her again.

"Better watch your step," he jeered. "Yoshitsune's probably cursing you for sitting on his precious rock."

Randy could almost hear the sound of the last straw snapping. She whipped around, snatched her arm free from his grasp and glared up into eyes that reminded her of frozen chunks of amber.

"If he's going to curse anyone, it'll be you," she snarled. "Now get the hell out of my way."

Dumb. Oh, she'd been dumb, dumb, *dumb*.
Randy called herself names as she walked down the

narrow road that ran past the future site of Sawa
Town. Here, a mile or two away from the hill, work
crews were busy clearing and leveling land.

At the moment, the area around the hill was un-
touched, but recalling the determined look in Ken
Sawa's eyes, Randy knew that this state of affairs
wouldn't last too long. In the absence of Junjiro, Ken
called the shots. If he said that Yui Hill would be destroyed, it would be destroyed. If he decreed that
Randy Muir would get no cooperation from him, that
was what was going to happen.

"You blew it, Muir," she growled at herself. "You
really blew it. Talk about unprofessional conduct. To
lose your temper like that at the one man who could
have been your ally— Lady, you take the prize."

The pity of it was that under other conditions, she
thought they could have worked well together. When
they'd first met, she'd liked both his humor and intelligence and thought him a very attractive man. And
he'd been intrigued by her, too. Randy hadn't lived for
twenty-seven years, even though twenty-three of them
had been spent in Kansas, without knowing when a
man was interested in getting to know her better.

A pebble the size of Mt. Rushmore had worked its
way into her shoe. Too dispirited to even stop to remove it, Randy hobbled on.

She'd spoiled everything by losing her temper. No
matter what the provocation, there'd been no excuse
for that. It wasn't like her, not like the Randy Muir
who prided herself on maintaining her cool under fire,
who during her apprentice years at the *Topeka Her-*

ald had taken jobs nobody else would touch with a ten-foot pole.

When she'd gone to New York to work for Hal Breeland at *Issues Today,* her first assignment had been a real winner—a foulmouthed, chauvinistic entrepreneur who'd made his billions by stepping on everyone around him. She'd managed *him,* yet fifteen minutes after having met Ken Sawa, she was cussing him out.

"Why?" she moaned aloud, then stopped short as an unlikely answer snaked its way into her mind. Perhaps she'd lambasted Ken because he reminded her of Nate Brady.

But she balked at this. Things were bad enough already without her drumming up her ex-fiancé. Instead of half-baked personal analysis, what she needed was to find a way to write about the Sawas without an interview.

She carried this depressing thought with her into the grounds of the Grand Hotel Asatsuki. In spite of its fancy name, the hotel was a small, squat building flanked by the tiniest of Japanese gardens. Even so, the uniformed doorman sprang to attention to open the immaculately scrubbed and polished glass door, and sang out a cheerful greeting. "Did the honored guest have a good walk?" he asked.

The question was repeated by the desk clerk, who bowed as he handed Randy her key, and by the chambermaid who passed her in the hall en route to her Western-style room. The room was tiny but comfortable, with a bed, a desk placed under a framed specimen of Japanese calligraphy and two chairs pulled close to the window so as to provide a ringside view of Yui Hill.

Randy sat down in one of the chairs, cast a brooding look at the hill and pulled out a file from her briefcase. Wriggling her feet free of shoes, she propped them up on the other chair and began to review her file on the Sawas.

Junjiro Sawa, the self-styled "shogun of modern industry," had started his career as an architect. He had made his fortune by building luxury hotels, business-shopping complexes and resorts. Among other things, he had designed a palace for an Arab prince, and a much-admired villa in Cannes for a film magnate.

Sawa Town was to be the culmination of a lifetime of building. The sixty-six-year-old industrialist-architect had taken years to plan this huge residential and commercial development, which was to be built on a large tract of land here in Asatsuki. As Randy had explained to her boss, Hal Breeland, it wasn't just the size and scope of Sawa Town, but *where* it was being built. A piece of traditional Japan, centuries old, was being sacrificed to one man's vision of progress.

There was a knock on the door, and a diminutive Japanese woman peered around the heavy door. "Ran-dee. I am intruding?"

"Minny!" Randy yelped.

Jumping to her feet, she ran toward the newcomer and hugged her. "It's good to see you, Minny! I thought you couldn't get away today."

"I had a class to teach in the morning, so I could not meet your plane." Minako apologized. She patted her friend's back as she added, "No one has called me 'Minny' since I say goodbye to you and your so-kind family. How are they?"

"Fine. Pete and Jill's baby girl is walking now, and Charlie got engaged last month. Doreen, Lysa and Helen are just great. Mom's gardening like mad, and Dad's still trying to get his golf score down. They all sent you tons of presents." Randy paused to draw breath and held her friend at arm's length. "You've lost weight," she accused.

In her high-school days, Minako had stood four foot ten in her stockinged feet and weighed in at ninety-two pounds. Now she looked even tinier. With jet black hair that hung to her waist and delicate features, Minako had the appearance of a porcelain doll. But Randy knew that Minny could be strong-minded, even downright stubborn at times.

Randy drew her friend toward the chairs by the window. "Is everything okay, Minny?"

"I am at the end of my wits." Minako sighed. "Professor Murano, our chief at Ohashi University, sent Junjiro Sawa several letters about Yoshitsune's tears—which is what the local people call *Ephemerum hygromatica*. There was no answer, so we held a demonstration outside the Sawa Building."

Listening to Minako's description of the demonstration, Randy gathered that it had been very orderly, very correct. Minny and her colleagues had carried signs and had marched politely around the Sawa Building.

"Junjiro Sawa was not here in Asatsuki when we demonstrated. He was at his home in Ashiya with some kind of virus, so his son is meeting with us. Ken Sawa has been educated in both Japanese and American schools all his life. He went to America to high school and college. He has the Western thinking. We hoped he would listen to us, but he said Yui Hill had to be destroyed to make way for a bank." Minako sighed. "We will demonstrate again, of course, but it is not a hopeful case."

The fatalism in her small friend's voice made Randy frown. "What you need is to make a lot of noise. Minny, do you remember the time my mom wanted to help old Mrs. McInto paint her house?"

Minako looked puzzled. "Of course, I am remembering. Your mother said she couldn't do it alone, so she is convincing your father, all your brothers and sisters *and* you and me to help. How hard we worked that day! But what has that to do with Yui Hill?"

"Have you ever heard the expression, 'together we stand, divided we fall'? The historical society doesn't want the hill destroyed any more than you do."

"But we are not knowing anyone from the historical society, Ran-dee."

Randy reached out to her files and withdrew an article. "It says in this UPI release that a Mr. Shin Naka is secretary of the society. Telephone the society office and ask to speak to him, Minny."

Minako looked horrified. "You mean now? Just telephone this Naka-san without an introduction? That is impolite. I cannot do such a thing. Besides, we cannot force the Sawas to do anything against their will. They are as powerful as tigers."

Randy thought of the high-handed way in which Ken had refused to give her an interview. She recalled the look in his eyes when he'd ordered her to keep away from his father.

"Tigers, huh?" she mused. "Let's rattle their cage and see what happens."

Chapter Two

From his fifth-floor office in the Sawa Building, Ken watched the demonstration take shape.

He didn't like what he saw. When he'd heard that the Ohashi University botanists were going to protest again, he hadn't given it much thought. He'd expected a rehash of their first demonstration—scholarly types marching with signs and banners, speeches broadcast over loudspeakers, a petition presented by a representative of the group. In short, a manageable nuisance.

What he now had on his hands was a full-blown mess. It had started in the early morning with the police cordoning off the entire block, and now rows of white-clad men and women were massed around the Sawa Building. Their headbands proclaimed them to be Historical Environmentalists, and they carried banners and signs that declared Traditional Values Are

The Treasure Of Japan, and Save Yoshitsune's Tears Lest We All Weep.

There had to be at least a hundred demonstrators, but they'd been smart enough to keep things orderly. So far there had been no incidents between them and the police or the Sawas' own security detail. Meanwhile, the media was having a field day. Television cameras, both national and local, had shown up as though this was the greatest show on earth. Representatives from the major papers were out there mingling with the protesters, and even Gin Kamakuni, a popular radio talk show host, had jumped on the bandwagon.

There was a diffident cough at Ken's elbow. "Kamakuni eats this sort of thing up. He's talking to the leaders now."

Ken saw that Goh Yamazaki had come to stand beside him at the window. A stout, balding little man with a whispery voice, Yama did not appear to be the type to be Sawa Industries's Asatsuki branch director, but there was no one in the firm who was more capable, loyal or more well-informed. "The woman is called Watanabe, and the man's name is Naka," he was saying. "He is a high school teacher and the secretary of the society."

Shin Naka was a bean pole of a man, so skinny as to be almost anorexic, and Watanabe was probably not even five feet tall. But she was making a lot of noise. Both she and Naka had bullhorns and were acting like cheerleaders, egging on the others and appealing to the spectators to join their cause.

"Now Kamakuni's talking to that Western woman," Yamazaki went on. "I wonder if she's a reporter for one of the international papers."

"She's a writer from *Issues Today*," Ken said grimly. He hadn't spotted Randy earlier, probably because she was wearing a white suit and blended in with the demonstrators. Ken frowned as he watched her speak into the microphone that Kamakuni held before her. He had no doubt where *her* sympathies lay.

"Yama," he said, "I'm going to go out and talk to these people."

Yamazaki looked alarmed, but before he could speak, someone coughed behind them. Murai, the senior department chief, asked deferentially, "Is that wise, sir? You could be harmed."

Turning from the window, Ken faced half a dozen pairs of concerned eyes. He had often wished that he'd pushed harder to get his father to adopt the Western custom of allowing the president and vice president of Sawa Industries private offices. As things stood, both Junjiro and his son had desks at the apex of an inverted U of other desks, each one arranged in order of its owner's rank.

"Murai-kun is right, sir," Yamazaki urged. "If you wait until the crowd calms down—"

"Emotions will only escalate, Yama. Those people need to know right now that Yui Hill isn't a negotiable issue."

As Ken started to leave the room, his staff shot to their collective feet. Everyone looked disappointed when Ken said, "Stay here, please. This mustn't look like a confrontation."

He left the office and strode toward the elevators while his branch manager trotted after him, pleading, "At least take me with you. What will I say to your honored father if I let you face that mob out there alone?"

"There's police and security out there, for heaven's sake. Trust me on this one, Yama. I know what I'm doing."

Obviously unhappy, Yamazaki remained where he was while Ken took the elevator to the ground-floor reception area. This area was usually humming with activity, but today it was empty. The pretty receptionist, her dark eyes a little scared, got to her feet and bowed deeply to Ken. He gave her a reassuring smile that turned to a frown as he neared the sliding glass doors.

There was quite a commotion as Ken Sawa stepped through the glass doors and onto the steps of the Sawa Building. Randy watched as, amid the yells, shouts and demands, he paused on the steps and deliberately looked about him. The man didn't look conciliatory, she observed. In fact, he looked downright arrogant.

With the air of a king about to convey an honor on his subjects, he descended the steps and made for the thin man with the bullhorn. "Are you the leader of these people?" he barked.

The thin young man pushed his spectacles higher on his nose and squared his narrow shoulders. "I am Shin Naka, of the Greater Kanto Historical Society," he announced. "I represent my group, the Historical Environmentalists. We are here because we want to stop you from—"

"If you expect me to listen to what you have to say," Ken cut in, "you had better present your list of demands through the proper channels. I promise to review them."

From the corner of his eye he'd observed Yamazaki hovering anxiously on the other side of the sliding glass doors. Then Ken's attention was claimed by the tiny woman leader. "We've already sent you a list of demands, Sawa-san," she snapped. "You ignored them."

From her position near the steps, Randy watched Ken turn slowly to face Minako. He looked at poor Minny as if she were some kind of interesting bug he'd found crawling along the ground, but he said nothing.

The silence was intimidating, insulting. Randy saw her friend falter. Don't let him fluster you, Minny, she thought.

Gathering up her courage, Minako continued, "We have met before, Sawa-san. I was with the group of botanists who begged you not to destroy a valuable moss. You refused to listen to us."

Ken saw Randy give the little woman a thumbs-up gesture of approval. His eyes narrowed slightly as he replied, "If I recall our meeting correctly, I offered to move the moss."

Minako raised her bullhorn to her lips and shouted, "*Ephemerum hygromatica* can't live anywhere but on Yui Hill. Moving it will kill it."

A roar of approval rose from the demonstrators, and Randy muttered, "The ball's in your court, mister."

Once she'd convinced Minny that all of Japan wouldn't collapse if she phoned Shin Naka, Minny had taken the ball and run with it. She and the thin history teacher had met and brainstormed. Minny had suggested the slogans and the new name for their joint group, and Shin had proposed that everyone dress in white, the traditional color of mourning. Then they'd started phoning environmental groups, schools, other historical societies, anyone who might listen and support their cause.

The result was a large, loud and highly effective public outcry worthy of the media coverage that had been Randy's idea. At Minny's request, she'd used her contacts to interest both local and national television stations, as well as the newspapers.

Ken Sawa should realize by now that he couldn't push everyone around. Randy noted, however, that he didn't look chastened as he said, "I'm sure you agree that the good of the group outweighs any personal consideration. A moss, no matter how rare, can't be held as important as the benefits that would accrue from Sawa Town." He rattled off the names of the large department stores, banks and business concerns that were going to be built in his father's new complex, and concluded, "Naturally there will also be a more modern hospital, schools and services for the people of Asatsuki."

Since Minny seemed to have been silenced by this glib speech, Randy raised her voice to ask, "Sawa-san, isn't it possible to build Sawa Town without destroying Yui Hill?"

She'd spoken in very passable Japanese. Out of the corner of his eye, Ken saw Gin Kamakuni hovering closer and knew that whatever answer he gave now would be quoted by housewives all over Japan.

"'Destroy' is a harsh word," Ken temporized.

Damn the woman. He'd almost succeeded in calming things down, but now the demonstrators were getting stirred up again. As he listened to their yells, Ken glared at Randy and saw that a lock of her dark, wavy hair had fallen forward against her cheek. The wholly illogical desire to push back that dark strand warred with an understandable urge to strangle her.

He snatched the bullhorn from Shin Naka's hand and shouted into it. "We at Sawa Industries realize what's at stake here. As vice president of the firm, I promise you that your demands are being given serious consideration. If the Historical Environmentalist group will select representatives, I will meet with them. Yamazaki-san, the director of our Asatsuki branch office, will make the arrangements for such a meeting."

A small, bald, mild-mannered man came hurrying down the steps of the Sawa Building. He bowed to the demonstrators, then to Shin and Minako. They both bowed back. Ken Sawa watched them with a satisfied smile, then turned to answer questions from the press.

Was that *it?* Randy glanced toward Shin and Minny, who were deep in conversation with Yamazaki. Behind her, the demonstration was breaking up. Though some of the younger people were still chanting their slogans, their fervor had gone. It was over, Randy thought, and Ken Sawa was going to walk away smelling like a rose.

"Ms. Muir, do you have a moment?"

She hadn't heard Ken come up behind her until he'd slid an arm through hers. As he marched her in the direction of the Sawa Building, he said, "I'm impressed."

He'd spoken in English, so she replied in kind. "What with?"

Though he was smiling for the benefit of the still-whirring TV cameras, Randy knew that this was one angry man. The muscles of his arm were taut, and she could almost feel his tension sear her through the fabric of his expensive Italian silk suit. "I didn't realize you had so much expertise in crowd control," he continued.

"Are you saying that this demonstration was *my* idea?"

"Wasn't it?"

They'd entered the Sawa Building. In that silent place his voice sounded unusually loud, and when he swung around to face her, Randy actually caught her breath at the expression in his eyes. "Neither the historical society nor the eggheads from Ohashi would have thought to join forces," he grated. "They'd never have been able to put together this morning's entertainment without help."

Carefully removing her arm from his, Randy said, "Thanks for the compliment, but I didn't help anyone. It was Minny's idea to demonstrate—"

"I'm sure you made a *few* suggestions."

He was interrupting her again. Randy's voice hardened as she replied, "Actually Minny and Shin Naka worked out the agenda themselves."

Ken thought of the tiny Japanese woman and the reedy young man he had confronted. He snorted. "In a pig's eye. You might be able to make moony-eyed idealists dance to your tune, but I warn you against trying that trick on me."

"Really."

"Really! If you write one word about Sawa Town, our attorneys will slap a libel suit on *Issues Today*."

They were standing scant inches apart. Randy remembered reading somewhere that Japanese people disliked standing too close to others. Ken Sawa not only didn't seem to mind, but he was using his formidable physique to intimidate her. She felt as though she were squaring up to an angry lion.

The atmosphere around them seemed charged, sulfurous, ready to explode. Randy's glands were shooting so much adrenaline into her body that her knees shook. "Are you *afraid* of what I might write?" she challenged.

She could see his powerful form actually quiver as he fought for control. "Your involvement in this demonstration is an example of the biased kind of article you'd write."

"And I've told *you* that I call the shots as I see them."

"For God's sake, woman," Ken shouted, "why can't you take no for an answer?"

He glared down at Randy, who glared back. Her green eyes like ice, she hissed, "Take your hands off me!"

Ken looked down and, to his horror, realized that he had grasped Randy's wrist. He dropped it hastily, but not before the warm silkiness of her skin had made its impact. He could feel that warmth, that silkiness, curl like perfumed smoke through his veins.

Randy Muir brought out the worst in him, Ken thought groggily. When she was goading him, he didn't behave like the civilized, cosmopolitan man he was, but reacted like one of his Viking forebears. Right now it would have been a relief to roar primitive challenges and throw furniture around.

Locking his hands behind his back, he growled, "Why can't you just go home?"

Once more their eyes clashed like drawn blades, and this time Randy's knees held firm. "No way, mister," she told him. "Not until I've done what I came here to do."

"I'm only a simple housewife," the middle-aged woman protested. "Why ask *me* about Sawa Town?"

"But you've lived near Yui Hill all your life, Fujimori-san," Randy persisted. "What do you think about Yui Hill being dynamited?"

Stubbornly the woman shook her head. "I have nothing to say."

The words were depressingly familiar. Randy suppressed a sigh and shut off her tape recorder. "Thank you," she said. "I appreciate the time you've taken to speak with me."

She bowed. Minako, who'd come along to help translate, bowed. Mrs. Fujimori bowed also and followed the younger women out through her old-fashioned stone entryway into the tiny garden outside. Here she paused to ask, "You are traveling with your husband, Muir-san?"

Randy shook her head. "I'm not married."

Surprise, curiosity and concern flitted rapidly over Mrs. Fujimori's broad face. "How old are you?" she inquired. When told, she lapsed into animated Japanese that was too swift for Randy to follow. "You should listen to me. You don't want to end up a Christmas cake," she concluded.

As they walked away from the little house, Randy asked, "What was all that about a cake?"

"Fujimori-san said that a twenty-seven-year-old woman shouldn't be single. She suggested that it is time you quit traveling and writing articles and start finding yourself a husband."

Randy began to laugh.

"You might as well get used to it, Ran-dee. Japanese people feel that every woman wants to get married. If you're not married by age twenty-five, many people consider you a 'Christmas cake.'"

"Say what?"

Minako explained that Christmas cakes left unsold after December 25 were considerably diminished in value. "It is slang for the old miss," she continued. "That is not good, so everyone tries to make a match for a single woman. The parents try. The relatives try. Friends and employers and even strangers try."

There was a note of dejection in Minako's voice.

"You sound as if you've had experience, Minny."

"My parents are always trying to set me up with *omiai*, or arranged dates. I tell them that I am a modern woman and have no use for such old-fashioned business." Minako looked gloomy. "My parents think I am crazy. They are always telling me that Japanese men are—how you say it?—threatened by the fact that I am an assistant professor of botany. I am nearly twenty-nine years old, so maybe they are right."

"Almost a candidate for a rocking chair, yet. Good grief, Minny—"

"I am rapidly going over the hills. So, I will not marry. I will be an old miss." Minako waved a hand as if dismissing the subject and added, "Never mind about that. What are you going to do about your interviews?"

Randy glanced ruefully down at her notepad. Of the twenty people she had approached today, only two had given an opinion about Sawa Town. "Looks like nobody wants to talk to me."

She had spent the past four days trying to discuss Sawa Town with the people of Asatsuki. It wasn't as easy as she'd thought it would be. Even though everybody knew about the demonstration and was familiar with the concerns of the Historical Environmentalists, the townspeople remained closemouthed.

Thinking that her imperfect knowledge of Japanese was at fault, Randy had asked Minako to go along as a translator. They had spent all morning together, but matters hadn't improved, and the one man who had been willing to talk with her had been solidly on the side of the Sawas. Anything Sawa-san did, he told

Randy severely, was all right by him. Why was she going around bothering people?

"You know why they won't speak to you, don't you?" Minako was asking now. "Ken Sawa is controlling the townspeople to stay silent."

"I wouldn't put it past him," Randy muttered. "Minny, I don't understand why you and Shin swallowed what he said at the demonstration. You should have kept on making noise till he gave you a real answer."

Minako looked unhappy. "We are in Japan, Randee. In this country, we dislike disharmony and confrontation. At least Ken Sawa promised to consider our position."

"Do you really believe that he'll honor that promise?"

"We do not know. The ball is in their courts. Randee, you must realize that whatever anyone does or says, Sawa Industries has the last words."

Minako had an afternoon class to teach, so Randy accompanied her to the train station. Later, walking back toward the town, Randy could see the Sawa Building looming ahead of her. It had been built several years ago, when Junjiro first conceived the idea of Sawa Town, and housed not only Sawa Industries but a bank, a prestigious law firm and several exclusive boutiques. Its sleek aluminum facade and central core of glass dominated Asatsuki, and Randy knew that Minny was right. Here in Asatsuki the Sawas would always have the last word.

Unless Ken Sawa gave his approval, the townspeople would not open up to her. And lacking both an interview and the cooperation of the townspeople, her article was snookered. Randy knew that her only chance to reverse matters was to talk to Ken, but she knew that he'd refuse even to hear her out.

Besides, she wasn't sure that she wanted to have another confrontation with him. The last time they'd gone nose to nose had left her more shaken than she cared to admit. Ken Sawa was different from anyone she'd met. He was intelligent and he was manipulative, an opportunist who could charm or intimidate so as to be in control of every situation.

Like Nate Brady— Randy frowned as that persistent thought resurfaced. Why did she keep comparing the two men? That part of her life was over. *"Finito,"* Randy muttered. *"Caput.* The end."

"Do you talk to yourself a lot?" said Ken at her elbow.

Randy gave a highly unprofessional start of surprise. "What are you doing here?" she demanded.

Instead of answering immediately, he looked her over, taking in her serviceable slacks and matching suit jacket, her blouse of amber silk. Over her shoulder was a large leather shoulder bag containing her tape recorder and other journalistic paraphernalia.

"You look like a woman on the move," he commented. "Talk to a lot of people this morning?"

"A few."

"I hope the interviews went well."

"I've had some interesting reactions."

She'd been determined not to rise to his bait, but his complacent expression made her want to kick him in the shins. With difficulty Randy remained silent until he volunteered, "I'm going to lunch. Care to join me?"

"Why?" she asked, suspiciously.

"Why not?"

Randy turned her head and stared hard at the man walking beside her. He was wearing an impeccably fitted gray suit, his shirt was snowy white, and there was a black pearl in the folds of his gray silk tie.

He looked pretty snazzy in a rich, understated way, and he didn't even resemble the angry and arrogant individual who had confronted her at the Sawa Building some days ago. Today Ken was coming across as pleasant and reasonable. He was smiling. With all her soul, Randy distrusted that smile.

But she also knew that she couldn't reject his invitation out of hand. Asatsuki was a small town. The minute she lunched with the boss-man, the word would be out, and by evening everyone in Asatsuki would think she'd been accepted by the ruling family.

Yes! Randy thought. Aloud she said, "I'd be delighted."

Ken's grin widened at her uncharacteristically prim reply, but all he said was, "Dai-suké's restaurant is on the corner."

Randy blinked with surprise to see the tiny shop he was gesturing at. Ken Sawa didn't look to be the type to patronize such a humble establishment.

He rattled open the sliding glass door and ushered her into a dark shop scented with delicious cooking smells. It was a tiny place with a row of tables and wooden chairs across a wall and a counter. All but one of the tables were occupied, and a dozen men and women were jostling for standing space at the counter while slurping soup and noodles out of big bowls. Still others waited their turn.

The master of the house stood behind the counter. He was giving an order to his woman assistant but broke off when he saw Ken. "Welcome, welcome, Sawa-san," he bawled. "What'll it be today?"

"The usual, Dai-suké," Ken called back. "And one for my guest."

Randy scanned the well-worn menu pasted to the back wall of the shop, but it was all written in Japanese. "What is 'the usual'?" she asked. "Not that it matters. Everything smells so good."

"Everything *is* good. Dai-suké and his wife do all their own cooking, and they're masters of noodle making. But *ten-don*—tempura over noodles—is the specialty of the house."

Two young men, dressed in dark business suits, had just vacated their places at the counter. Immediately two more customers took their places. "Do we line up?" Randy wondered.

"No need. Dai-suké keeps a table for me."

He led the way to the one unoccupied table. "Rank has its privileges," Randy observed dryly.

"Dai-suké, his wife, Mari-san, and I are old friends." Ken smiled his thanks at a grinning little woman who slapped down chopsticks, a teapot and teacups on the table. "Have a little tea to clear your palate," he advised.

Before she could take his advice, two huge earthenware bowls brimming with tempura, thick white noodles and soup were placed before them. Randy tried a small slurp and found it delectable. The broth was beautifully flavored, and the noodles firm and fresh. The shrimp tempura, nestled on top of the noodles, was the crispest and hottest she'd ever tasted.

For a few minutes they savored the good food in silence. Then Ken asked, "Learn anything interesting from your interviews?"

Randy's mouthful of soup and noodles almost went the wrong way. "Not a whole lot," she admitted.

"You can't blame people for not wanting to talk to a stranger. They're probably afraid you might twist their words around."

"That's simply not true." Randy pushed her bowl aside to add earnestly, "You think I'm biased because Minny is my friend, don't you? If you've read any of my published articles—"

He interrupted her. "I have."

She blinked. "You—you have? Then you must see that I don't editorialize on one side of an issue." He made no comment, and she added earnestly, "I've done my homework on Sawa Industries. I have a great deal of respect for your father's vision. I appreciate your position. That's why I'd like to *hear* your position for my article."

The sincerity in her voice was unfeigned. Her frankness was like a friendly hand offered across the table. For a moment Ken found himself actually wishing that he could explain his position.

Instead, he said, "Have some tea. It's soothing to the nerves."

He'd been on the point of softening—she knew it. Perhaps all wasn't lost after all. Randy persisted, "I want to write a fair-minded story. I'd like to show that Sawa Town is a symbol of everything that has made Japan successful."

"But at the same time you believe that tradition is more important than progress," he pointed out. "Why not come out and admit it?"

"Because what I may or may not personally feel isn't the issue. I want to show both sides of what's happening here. But if neither you nor the townspeople talk to me, I can't do that." Randy paused. "Look, if you're concerned that my interviewing technique isn't fair, you can contact the people I spoke with. I can give you their names."

He said, "I know who you've spoken to."

"Do you mean you've had me *followed?*" she gasped.

"You've been watching too many mysteries. Asatsuki's a small town and news travels. You ought to know that, being a Meldon girl."

On top of everything, the man had a good memory. And he was sharp. Reluctantly Randy grinned and admitted, "That's why I had lunch with you today."

Ken hadn't expected her to be so forthright, but then Randy Muir was constantly surprising him. For instance, there were her interviewing tactics. Instead of trying to influence anyone, she'd apparently bent over backward to be as fair as possible.

Fair and honest and tough-minded. With or without his help, she was going to write her article. The problem was that negative publicity about Sawa Town in a well-known magazine like *Issues Today* would cast a slur on Junjiro Sawa's name.

He couldn't allow that. Abruptly Ken decided to follow through on the plan that had been forming in his mind. "Do you have any appointments after lunch?" he asked.

"A couple of interviews, but I can cancel them." A wild hope leapt into Randy's breast. "Do you mean— are you going to give me that interview?"

"I'm going to do something much better than that." Ken leaned across the table and captured Randy's hand in his. "If you come with me, I'll show you Happiness."

Chapter Three

"You'll show me *what?*"

Snatching her hand away as if it'd been scalded, Randy stared hard at Ken, who explained, "'Happiness' is a living complex for our married employees. What did you think I meant?"

Behind that look of feigned innocence, she was positive he was laughing at her. There was frost in her voice as she demanded, "Why would I be interested in Hap—in this place?"

"First I want to tell you that I've enjoyed your articles, especially the one that came out this January about child labor in the States. The research alone must have taken some time."

The sincerity in Ken's tone caused Randy's indignation level to subside somewhat. "Yes, it did," she agreed.

The child-labor piece had been hard to write. The workers had been afraid to talk to her, the owners of the sweatshops had been hostile. Worst of all, Randy recalled the sick feeling she'd had when she'd seen those sad-eyed little kids huddled over sewing machines. She'd had to fight the urge to scoop them all up and take them home with her.

"I couldn't believe at first that such things happened in this day and age," she told Ken. "Yet in the States there's been a hundred-and-fifty-percent increase in child-labor violations during the last six years."

"Since you obviously feel deeply for children, I know you'll be interested in seeing Happiness." Ken got to his feet. "Ready?"

As Randy rose also, a customer squeezed by and unintentionally jostled her. She fought for balance, failed, and fell forward against Ken. For an instant she registered the hard wall of his chest, the strength of arms that were supporting her. A hard chest, whipcord-lean waist, the press of hard thighs—

Hastily Randy moved away, but the effects of their brief contact remained. Under protective layers of clothing, her skin was teased with goose pimples. Get real, you ninny, she lectured herself.

Aloud she said, "Sorry about that. How do we get to, ah, Happiness?"

He could think of a few ways right off the bat. In the brief second he'd held Randy, Ken had registered every physical nuance about her. Her slender body had fit against him as if it were tailor-made to nestle against his, and her subtle perfume had tantalized him. His chest still felt the press of her firm breasts. In fact, he had the desire—no, it was an actual, physical need—to pull her back into his arms.

The intensity of that need astonished Ken. It wasn't his style. Though no playboy, he'd hardly lacked female companionship. Until last autumn, when Junjiro fell ill and the responsibility for Sawa Town had fallen on his shoulders, he'd been seeing the beautiful, intelligent daughter of a French diplomat. Yet neither Yvette—now back in Paris—nor any of his past liaisons had affected him as Randy Muir did. One fragmentary, accidental embrace, for God's sake, and he was as shaken as an adolescent mooning over his first love.

Perhaps the business of Sawa Town was getting to him. "We'll take the company car," Ken said. "I told the driver to meet me at Dai-suké's at one-thirty."

When they emerged from the shop into the bright sunlight, a luxury sedan, complete with uniformed chauffeur, stood waiting. At the sight of Ken, the man bowed deeply and opened the back door. Ken stepped aside to let Randy pass, and her arm brushed his. Hastily, aware that her treacherous skin still tingled with awareness and memory, she climbed into the car and sank against the plush seats.

"How far do we have to go to the apartment complex?" she asked as Ken joined her in the back seat.

"It's just outside Asatsuki. But it's a *living* complex, not just an apartment." Ken turned slightly in his seat beside her so that his knee touched hers. "An interesting distinction, don't you agree?"

Under the pretext of pulling out her pocket tape recorder, Randy managed to scoot a few inches away from the disturbing man next to her. "Do you object to my recording our conversation?" she asked in her most professional voice. "So, can you tell me what makes Happiness so special?"

Special was the word for her, all right. In this enclosed space, the subtle perfume she wore was intoxicating, and her lips were rosy and sweetly curved, an invitation to any man under a hundred and ten. Ken found it increasingly hard to resist that invitation as he replied, "I prefer you to see it for yourself. There's nothing like hands-on discovery."

The images that leapt to her mind had to be X-rated. Before Randy could deal with them, Ken commented, "The sun's on your side. Does it get in your eyes?"

She made the mistake of glancing up and seeing that *his* eyes were molten gold. The heat they generated probably could have vaporized a glacier. Hurriedly Randy turned her head to stare out of the window and saw that they were passing the site of the future Sawa Town. The clearing work was progressing steadily, and tractors, earth-movers and other machinery were advancing inexorably on Yui Hill.

The sight of the hill acted like a much-needed antidote. "Why did you choose Asatsuki as the site for Sawa Town?" she questioned.

"You know what they say about location," he replied. "We wanted Sawa Town to be an easy commute from Tokyo."

Her voice had turned cool and professional again, and Ken welcomed the change. There was no percentage—no *sense*—in becoming involved with someone like Randy Muir. Silently he reminded himself just why he was taking her to see the Happiness complex.

"As for Yui Hill," he continued, "we regret having to destroy it, and we've decided to erect a shrine to Yoshitsune right in Sawa Town. Besides pacifying the historical society, it'll draw tourists and be good for business."

Before she could react to this, Happiness came into view. Randy wasn't overly impressed with the tall, gray, narrow building, which was set on huge cinder blocks and reminded her of a young child's creation.

But if Happiness was downright homely, it was also spotlessly clean. Three young women were outside sweeping as the sedan drove up. "Sawa-san, welcome," one of them called. "Will you and your guest have some tea?"

"No, thank you, we've just come to look around. My guest is a writer, and wants to learn more about Happiness," Ken replied politely. He led Randy around the cinder-block building, adding, "That was Enoshima-san, who heads the grounds committee."

"She's doing a good job." Randy looked appreciatively at a Japanese garden with a stone lantern, carefully pruned trees and a small pond full of water lilies. The garden's air of serenity somehow made Happiness appear less ugly. As she followed Ken into the building, Randy remarked, "My mother's a gardener, and so is my sister Lysa. They're outside all the time, digging and weeding. Mom says a house is not a home without a garden."

Ken nodded. "We wanted the Happiness building to feel like home to the families of our employees."

"You're talking about relocation, aren't you?"

"Relocation is a cold word, Randy. We're talking about quality of life here."

As Ken spoke, they stepped through swinging doors into a large entryway. Here they replaced their shoes with felt slippers, and Ken led the way into a hallway that was bare except for a large, centrally placed table. On the table was a diorama of the future Sawa Town.

With Ken's permission Randy snapped several photographs. Though she'd seen the blueprints and some drawings of Sawa Town during her research, she was impressed by the grace and power conveyed by the diorama. It had a device that would light up any given building, and she spent some time identifying the various structures that would one day grace Sawa Town. There were three department stores, a cooperative market, a hospital fronted by a park complete with flower garden and fountains. Next to the park there was a bank that would be built over the rubble of Yui Hill.

In her mind Randy tried to move the bank somewhere else, but found that she couldn't do so without altering the entire concept of Sawa Town. She was deep in thought when Ken, who had been standing by silently while she looked over the diorama, broke in. "Let me give you the ten-cent tour," he said.

The tour was impressive. On the first floor several classes were in session. In one room women were learning flower arrangement, and an ebullient cooking class was in session next door. There were martial-arts classes, foreign-language classes. And on the next floor, Randy found a spotless nursery decorated in sunshiny colors. Here, motherly attendants watched over rows of sleeping infants.

"Women, as well as men, work at the construction site," Ken explained. "Others hold clerical jobs with our company or are office ladies. The married ones feel confident that their children are cared for. Of course, we have a nurse and a pediatrician standing by."

Randy watched a motherly woman holding a baby and singing to it. The baby had a sleepy look of contentment and the woman looked happy, too. "Isn't it unusual for a firm to be so concerned about its workers' families?" she asked.

"A happy worker is a good worker. Besides, family loyalty is one of the most important Confucian virtues." Ken grinned. "I believe in some traditions, obviously."

Only when it serves your interests— But she didn't say the words aloud. Instead, Randy thought of her brothers and sisters. All of them were scattered, now, with only Pete and Lysa living near the folks. But if one of them was in trouble, everyone came flocking home.

"Americans believe in family, too," she told Ken. "At least, the Muirs do. Mom and Dad were the kind of parents that gave us kids roots and wings. We all go our own way, but we're very close."

"In Japan there's no such thing as 'going your own way,'" Ken commented.

She was about to ask him why not when they came to a room filled with toddlers. The tots, who ranged in age from two to four, were doing calisthenics to the tune of a tinkling piano. Ken opened the door to the sunny room, and the woman who was playing the piano announced, "It's Sawa-san and a guest. Group, what do we say?"

Immediately the toddlers lined up, placed their hands on their knees and bowed. *"Kon-nichi-wa,"* they chanted. Randy knew this meant "hello."

One tiny little girl with stiff pigtails and a big pink bow on top of her head was so chubby that she nearly fell over when she bowed. She stared at Randy, put her hands to her mouth and giggled. Randy ached to hug her.

"Don't let us disturb you," Ken said. "We've just come to watch you do your exercises."

"Why don't you join us, Sawa-san?" one of the older boys suggested, and their teacher smiled.

"They remember your last visit. You joined us then," she said.

Randy stared as Ken took off his jacket and tossed it over a chair. He loosened his tie, removed his cuff links—he actually has *cuff links,* Randy thought—and rolled up his shirtsleeves. Then he took his place in line. "All right, *Sensei,"* he said to the teacher, "I'm ready."

The piano started up again, and the children began to stretch and bend to its catchy beat. So did Ken. He appeared relaxed and unselfconscious, as though he were enjoying himself. Randy pulled out her camera and began to snap shots until the woman at the piano invited, "Why don't you join us, too?"

When in Rome— Besides, it looked like fun. Pausing only to set down her camera and remove her suit jacket, Randy joined the group.

"Enjoying yourself?" Ken asked after a while.

Randy nodded. "It loosens you up, you know? It makes me feel as if I'm back in Meldon, playing with my brother Pete's baby. I sure miss that little girl."

Ken said, "Family is what Happiness is all about." She was nodding agreement when he added, "It's a far cry from those kids in sweatshops."

Randy looked hard at Ken, trying to read the deceptively candid expression in his eyes.

Just a few days ago, Ken Sawa had practically ordered her to pack her bags and go home. Now he was falling over backward to be nice to her. Maybe he'd changed his mind about her after reading her articles, but she doubted that. More likely he'd decided that he couldn't scare her off, and so was now trying to influence her thinking. If she was going to write about Sawa Town, Ken was going to make sure she'd write what *he* wanted her to.

Randy's delicate brows drew together in a frown. Ken was an extremely attractive man, and as devious as they came, but she was no pushover. She'd been trained by the master manipulator of all time and knew all the tricks.

Aloud she said, "I'm impressed."

"You'll be even more impressed tomorrow," he told her.

Eyes narrowed in instinctive suspicion, she asked, "What about tomorrow?"

"Tomorrow I'm taking you on the Romance Car."

Happiness and Romance. No doubt they'd be visiting Love and Marriage next. As if he'd read Randy's thoughts, Ken grinned. "Nothing like that," he assured her.

He reached across to brush a curl of dark hair away from her cheek. The touch of his fingers on her skin was like a low-voltage electric shock.

"Romance is the railway name for the train to Hakone. I can't have you thinking that Asatsuki's all there is to Japan, can I? Tomorrow I'm taking you sight-seeing."

It had to be the slowest train in the world.

Randy had no idea how long they had been rattling about on the uphill tracks, but it felt as though it had been hours. As the train slowed, she asked hopefully, "Are we coming to Gora?"

"Not yet. Relax, Randy, and enjoy the scenery."

She didn't want to enjoy any more scenery. Her stomach felt queasy, and the way the train crawled up the mountains had reactivated a dormant fear of heights. It hadn't been bad when they were lower down, but as the mountains grew higher, she grew more and more uncomfortable.

She winced as the train jolted to a stop, and an old lady across the aisle smiled encouragingly and murmured, *"Shikari, shikari!"*

Get a hold of yourself—be strong. "I thought Gora was only ten miles from Odawara." Randy sighed.

The journey to Hakone-Yamato had been quite pleasant. The Sawa sedan had picked her up at her hotel early this morning and driven her and Ken into Tokyo. They'd taken the so-called Romance Car at Shinjuku Station. Sleek, modern and fast, the train had soon left the bewildering noise of Shinjuku behind, and Randy had enjoyed both the view through the large viewing windows and Ken's running commentary on the scenery.

They'd even glimpsed the white cone of Mt. Fuji peering out of the clouds. "You're in luck," Ken had commented. "Fuji-san's usually hidden at this time of year."

Unlike the temperamental mountain, Ken was in high spirits today. His travelogue was amusing and spiced with anecdotes that intrigued Randy or made her laugh. He'd also mentioned that he had come every summer to Kawaguchi, one of Hakone's five lakes, when he was a boy. "We had a house on the lake," he'd explained.

Had Junjiro actually had time to spare for his family? Apparently not. "My father was busy with his work," Ken explained, "so Nora—my mother—and I came here together. At least I did until I was nine."

Randy recalled that Ken must have been about nine when Nora Helgar had crashed near the Japanese Alps. She hoped he'd talk more about her, but he only added, "Later, Mrs. Yamazaki and her children accompanied me."

Randy remembered the chubby, balding man she'd seen during the demonstration. "Mr. Yamazaki is your Asatsuki director?"

"Yes. Yama has been with the family a long time."

Randy was intrigued that he had said "family" instead of "firm" but had no time to comment, for they had reached Hakone-Yamato and her troubles had begun.

Ken had suggested that they go on to Odawara then take the Hakone Tozan Tetsudo Line for Gora. "You'll like the view as we go over the mountains," he'd insisted.

She wasn't much for heights, but the distance seemed paltry, so she'd gone alone with his suggestion. Now she wished she hadn't been so trusting. The views *were* wonderful, but the train's pace was snail-like. In fact, it was amazing that it could climb at all.

"Don't worry, there won't be any accidents," Ken explained cheerfully. "The train uses three switchbacks. I'm a survivor of several trips on this good old train."

Randy shut her eyes as the good old train lurched to a stop on the steep slope. She kept them closed until it started again. When they approached yet another station, Randy was nearly desperate. "We're only at Chokoku-no-mori?" she groaned.

Ken took pity on her. "Would you like to get out and look around?"

Before he'd even finished asking, she was on her feet and practically sprinting for the door. "You're sure you don't want to go on to Gora?" he asked when he'd followed her onto the sun-washed platform.

"No way," she exclaimed, then laughed at herself.

He liked her spirit. He also liked the way her eyes turned to a softer green when she laughed. A stray sunbeam was touching the corners of her mouth, and for a moment he almost regretted subjecting her to that plaguey train. But, he reminded himself, he'd been trying to prove a point.

"Are you hungry?" he asked. "There's a Japanese inn about a quarter of a mile from here. Last time I was here they served decent food."

The way she felt now, she never wanted to eat again. Randy started to say so, then changed her mind. If she refused a meal, Ken might suggest they go on to Gora after all.

"I could go for some Japanese tea," she said cautiously.

An incipient sense of queasiness caused her to sway as they left the station, and he put an arm around her shoulders for support. He could feel her body ease against his, nestle close for a second before she tensed and drew away. "It's okay," she said. "I'm fine."

Was she reassuring him or herself? Ken wondered. It wasn't only that she was moving away from him, but she seemed to be pulling into herself. When he glanced down at her, he saw that there was a shadowed look in her eyes.

Her eyes were like spring leaves that had been bruised and crushed. He'd never seen her wear that expression before, and he didn't care for it. He was used to looking on Randy as a capable, take-charge woman with a mulish streak a mile wide. Why, suddenly, did she have to appear vulnerable?

Randy was thinking that she needed to be on her guard. Perhaps because of her temporarily weakened condition, she was more than ever conscious of Ken's charm. In spite of that awful train ride, she'd been enjoying his company. And then just now, when he'd put his arm around her, she'd felt—

Never mind what she'd felt. She hadn't come with Ken to *feel* anything. She was here to work. Randy reminded herself that when he'd suggested the sightseeing trip yesterday, she'd known two truths simultaneously. One was that this was a heaven-sent opportunity to get an informal interview with Ken. The second thing was that he was definitely up to something and that she had to be on her guard.

She kept her distance from him as they walked down a narrow road edged with pine and thickets of bamboo. The wind rustled through the bamboo and made a soft, hushing noise, and in the near distance a songbird sang. "It's so quiet," Randy murmured. "I can almost imagine myself back in time. Wouldn't it be great if a samurai warrior came galloping down this road?"

As she spoke, a truck, radio blaring, rounded the corner and came hurtling toward them. Ken grabbed Randy's arm and dragged her to safety, commenting, "The samurai acted as if they owned the road, too."

They turned off the main road and began to walk down a carefully tended side-path. At the end of the pathway stood the inn. Randy noted that it was a larger and much more elaborate version of the wooden, slate-roofed houses she'd seen at Asatsuki.

"The name of the inn is Kin Take Ya, or the Inn of the Gold Bamboo," Ken explained as they walked through the gate into an austerely beautiful Japanese garden. Ahead of them was an open wooden door curtained by purple cloth patterned with bamboo etched in gold thread. Pushing aside the cloth, they stepped into an old-fashioned entryway. A large, rectangular block of stone served as a step to the tatami-matted room above.

Ken called a greeting, and a dimpled young woman came hurrying up, dropped to her knees on the mats and bowed. "Welcome, honored guests," she cried. "Please, please come inside."

Following Ken's lead, Randy removed her shoes and slipped her feet into the slippers offered her by the maid. "Is the Nightingale Room free?" Ken was asking. Assured that it was, he added, "We want lunch served there."

The maid led them down a corridor made of wood so polished it glowed like dark silk, then knelt to slide open a wood-and-paper door. The Nightingale Room was small by Western standards and furnished only with a low table of some gleaming wood surrounded by flat, square cushions. On one side of the room was a raised section ornamented by a scroll covered with flowing Japanese calligraphy. In front of the scroll stood pine and iris arranged in a lacquer vase.

The maid pattered across the tatami and pulled open the wood-and-paper doors to disclose a miniature garden. A single Japanese maple, an arrangement of rocks and a tiny waterfall conveyed a feeling of tranquility.

"Satisfied with the room?" Ken wanted to know.

"It's perfect. But please don't order too much lunch, Ken, I'm not hungry." As the maid hurried away, Randy asked, "Why is this called the Nightingale Room?"

"The story is that one of the great haiku masters stayed the night. He didn't have any money, so he paid his bill with a poem about a nightingale. There it is on that scroll."

The dark flow of the Japanese characters was like a poem in itself. Randy was wishing that she'd learned to read Japanese as well as speak it, when Ken spoke behind her.

"'In the night silence/ the song of a nightingale./ Ah, my long-lost love.'"

Randy shivered involuntarily as Ken read the poem. He was standing so close to her that she could feel the warmth of his breath caress her cheek. If she took a step back, she would be in his arms.

She wanted to put some distance between them, but her legs wouldn't cooperate. Her tongue felt heavy, unable to form words that would defuse this dangerous moment. Silence throbbed between them like a shared heartbeat. Then, as though impelled to do so, she turned to look up at him.

Nothing that had ever happened to him had prepared Ken for the look in Randy's eyes. Liquid, luminous, they spoke to him more surely than could any words. He caught his breath and took a step toward her.

There was the sound of the screen opening, and the maid's cheerful voice cried, "Apologies for making you wait! This is country fare, but please try and eat it."

Randy blinked unseeing as the maid and a helper carried in trays of food. She felt dazzled as though she'd been staring into the white heat of the sun. When Ken touched her arm, she literally jumped.

"Shall we sit down?" Ken was grateful that his voice didn't betray the emotions that were still searing him. Needing a diversion, he began to tease the younger maid about her resemblance to one of TV's hottest pop singers.

Randy listened to Ken's cheerful banter with the maids and was disgusted with herself. A little poetry, the right setting, and she'd melted into a gob of Silly Putty. Another moment, and she would've been in his arms.

If you come with me, I'll show you happiness—

Randy lowered herself down on one of the cushions and forced herself to concentrate on the food before her. A red lacquer bowl held clear soup; a blue porcelain bowl offered matchstick slices of carrot, white radish and cucumber dressed subtly with sugar and vinegar; and a fish, complete with head and round, glazed eye, lay staring at her.

Just looking at that fish did unspeakable things to her digestive system, but she could probably manage the soup. Perhaps a combination of motion sickness and lack of food was causing the lightness in her brain. Cautiously Randy tried a sip of the soup and found it soothing. She drank it all and then nibbled on the salad. By the time she'd finished it, she realized she was hungry.

The second course—a helping of cold buckwheat noodles in a basket, hot tempura served with delectable sauce—went down easily. "This is delicious," Randy exclaimed.

"You'd better save enough room for the next course," Ken warned. "The specialty of the house is Kobe beef. It's so tender that you're supposed to be able to cut it with your chopsticks."

"*More* food?"

"You know what they say. An hour from now you'll be hungry again." Ken grinned. "I'm glad you've recovered from your ride this morning."

Randy was saved from answering by the maids, who brought in plates of beef and bowls of rice along with a basket of fresh fruit. When they had bowed themselves out, Ken continued, "I hope you enjoyed the train. After all, it's the traditional way to view the mountains."

Randy narrowed her eyes. "You're a devious man, Ken Sawa."

"I don't know what you're talking about."

"Like fun you don't. Yesterday you take me to see the Happiness building, and today you make me suffer on that medieval train. If you're trying to influence my thinking, you're wasting your time."

"Is that what I'm doing?"

"Well, aren't you?"

Instead of answering her, Ken reached into the basket and picked up a golden globe. "Try one of these Japanese pears," he invited. "They're a specialty here in this area. Nora used to love them."

Randy was torn between the wish to pin him down and the desire to learn more about his family. She looked up, saw the glint in his eyes and realized that this was exactly what he'd intended. Okay, she thought. She'd go with the flow and see what happened.

"Your mother died when you were nine or thereabouts," she said. "Forgive me for asking, but why didn't your father ever remarry?"

"We never discussed it, but I suspect it was because he was very involved with Sawa Industries. My uncles and aunt had invested heavily in the firm, and my father had the responsibility of protecting their assets."

"You mean that he had to think of his family first," Randy said. When Ken nodded, she continued. "But weren't his own needs important, too?"

"Not as important as his duty to the family." Looking unusually serious, Ken continued, "Japanese are raised with the concept of duty. It's a part of the old samurai code."

Randy wished that she could turn on her tape recorder, but was afraid that it would break the mood. Praying that she'd remember each word Ken said, she asked, "What about you, personally? What happens if your family's thinking happens to be in conflict with your own?"

An odd expression seemed to flicker in his eyes a moment before he began to laugh. "You're asking what happens when an irresistible force comes up against an immovable object. Still hungry?"

"Are you kidding? I doubt if I can even move. But going back to what you were saying—"

Ken raised a hand in a gesture of surrender. "Give me a break, will you please? It's a topic that has been around a long time. Books and two Kabuki plays have been written on samurai and *giri-ninjo*."

"Which is?"

"*Ninjo* is the principle of pleasure. *Giri* is duty or fealty. On one hand, the poor samurai wanted to please himself and enjoy life. On the other, there was his duty to his liege lord. The poor fellow was caught between a rock and a hard place."

Randy was about to ask what happened to modern-day samurai when Ken got to his feet. "I'm too full to do any heavy thinking," he told her. "What we both need is exercise. If you don't want to get back on the train right away, we could walk around town."

When she agreed gratefully, he came around the table and held out a hand to help her up. Randy was mentally rehashing what Ken had said and was wondering how she could get him back on the subject. It took her by surprise when he swung her to her feet and into the circle of his arms.

The movement was swift, unexpected. It seemed to astonish Ken almost as much as it did her. For a second they stared at each other. And then, as though it were the most natural thing in the world, he lowered his lips to hers.

Chapter Four

The press of his body against hers—hard wall of chest, flat, hard belly, hard imprint of thighs—contrasted with the gentleness of his lips. Wrapped in silk and steel, Randy breathed in Ken's distinctive scent and registered the tender-tough rasp of his cheek against hers.

Internal shock waves were rippling through her, and she half recognized them as warning flares. Some overworked, half-forgotten instinct, activated by danger, was urging her to break contact with Ken before any more damage was done to her reasoning circuitry. She tried to heed this sound advice, but found she couldn't move.

Through a tangle of his runaway emotions, Ken felt Randy relax in his arms. She was as tantalizing as hot wine, and her slender yet rounded body filled his arms as no other woman had before. Her skin was like peach-bloom satin, and her hair like finest silk. He'd fantasized about the taste of her lips since that first day on Yui Hill—

Ken didn't want to think of that wretched place, but it was too late. As his mind returned to Yui Hill, the desire that had obscured his thinking lifted like morning fog. Kissing Randy wasn't what he'd intended when he brought her out here. Though definitely pleasurable, kisses would do nothing to help his cause.

Dimly Randy realized that Ken had stopped kissing her. Her eyes flickered open as she heard him say, "You're entirely welcome."

"Huh?"

"I always liked the American custom of saying 'thank you' with a kiss," Ken said. "I'm glad you enjoyed the food."

He was smiling. He thought she'd been *thanking* him. Randy fumbled for something witty to say, but all her thoughts seemed to have left town. She realized that Ken was still holding her, his hands clasped loosely behind the small of her back. She was glad he was, since her legs felt quite boneless.

Cheerfully he continued, "We can take that walk now if you like."

She'd have *liked* to have been able to breathe properly. Her heart was still hammering. She felt as if she'd been running a marathon, for crying out loud, and here he was talking about a walk.

Then she told herself not to be foolish. It wasn't as if she'd never been kissed before. To show Ken—and herself—that she was hip and cool, Randy smiled and looked directly into Ken's eyes.

"A walk," she said heartily. "Sure. Fine. Sounds just great."

She knew that she was going to have to watch her step. She was here in Japan to write an article. She hadn't come halfway around the world to get involved with a modern-day shogun's son.

"So what do you think about this Ken Sawa?" Minako wanted to know.

It was two evenings later, and they were sitting in the lobby of the Asatsuki Grand Hotel. All day Minako had accompanied Randy around town, interpreting for her. This time people had been willing to talk, and to celebrate a string of successful interviews, Randy had invited Minako for a victory dinner.

"Ken's an interesting man," Randy said. "He's trying to prove to me that my ideas of Japan are all wrong."

"You mean that he is being crafty and sneaky?"

"No, more like manipulative. He's almost as good at it as Nate was."

The name had slipped out before she could hold it back, and Minny pounced at once. "Ah-hah, I see. You are speaking of the man to whom you were engaged. The handsome financier."

Her grin was so triumphant that Randy had to smile back. "Yes," she replied, then hastened to add, "So, what are you and Shin Naka up to these days?"

Minako began to relate the efforts of the Historical Environmentalists. Both she and Naka-san had been interviewed by the press. Interest in their cause was growing among historical groups and environmental clubs, and schoolchildren and their teachers as far as Kobe and Hokkaido had sent letters of support. In case the Sawas did not back down from their determination to destroy Yui Hill, there was talk of holding another demonstration.

"But we hope that it will not come to that," Minako concluded. "A meeting between Ken Sawa and us has been arranged by Mr. Yamazaki. Now, tell me, is Ken Sawa reminding you of Nate Bra-dee?"

Randy stifled a sigh. Like many Japanese, Minako felt that just as her own life was an open book, her friends should have no secrets from her. "Maybe," she hedged.

"You are writing me to say you and Nate were engaged after graduation from college," Minny prodded. "Why didn't you marry?"

"Because we were both busy with our careers. Nate had joined Fortham and Sloan, one of the most prestigious investment companies in the Midwest, and I'd just been hired by the *Topeka Herald*."

"That is modern and satisfactory," Minny said approvingly.

"One of the stories I covered around that time was about a multimillionaire whose marriage had gone on the rocks. Nate used that incident to point out how wise we were not to look at marriage in an old-fashioned way. He then suggested—do you know what a prenuptial agreement is, Minny?"

After she'd agreed to the prenuptial, they had set their wedding date. Randy had wanted a wedding back in Meldon with all the uncles and aunts and cousins attending. She'd wanted to be married in the church where her parents had exchanged vows, and to have the reception held in the same hall where her nervous Uncle Lewis had spilled champagne all over the happy couple. She'd put the matter to Nate somewhat diffidently—he'd been talking about a much different, much more stylish reception—and was touched when he agreed to do it her way. Only later had she realized that he'd sacrificed a battle so that he could win the war.

"Nate said he'd been doing a lot of thinking," Randy told Minako. "The way he put it was that we had only so many productive years. Children were an inconvenience during these years, so could we agree to put off having a family? Soon after that talk he started introducing me to happy, brilliant, successful couples on a career track. Nate pointed out that these couples had opted not to have children at all."

Randy had rebelled against any discussion of a childless marriage. Nate had calmed her down, sent roses, courted her with tenderness and passion. Because she'd loved him so much, she'd almost believed that she could live with his terms. Then, her sister-in-law had given birth to the clan's first grandchild, and holding that tiny morsel in her arms, Randy had realized what Nate was asking her to give up.

"So you sent back his ring." As Randy nodded, Minako said somberly, "I am thinking that it is better to be a Christmas cake like me than to be married to such a manipulative man. A person must not compromise what is deepest." She pressed a dainty hand to her heart as she added, "Naka-san so admires you."

"Ah—he does?"

"Naka-san," Minako said firmly, "is a traditional Japanese man. In many ways he and I are not agreeing on issues of women's place in society. But I admire him for so believing in Yoshitsune's Rock, and he admires *you*. You have the principles. You are not a shove-over for the Sawas."

Just then the night clerk came hurrying over to tell Randy that she had a phone call. When she went to the reception desk and picked up the receiver, a familiar deep voice spoke in her ear. "I'm sorry to be calling so late. Am I disturbing you?"

Naturally he wasn't disturbing her. Surprise at hearing from him had made her pulse beat more swiftly, that was all. "No—no, that's all right," Randy said hastily. "Is there something I can do for you?"

"That depends. Are you free tomorrow?"

"I'd have to check my schedule," she parried. "Why do you ask?"

"I'm going to Osaka on business and thought you might enjoy a ride on the *shinkansen*."

Randy thought about it. The *"shin"* was the much-touted bullet train, and she'd wanted to ride it just for the experience. She also needed to ask Ken several more questions. The ride to Osaka would take a few hours, and he would be a captive audience.

"I'd like that," she said.

"Good." Over the wires she could almost see him smile. No, she could *feel* it, the slow curve of his firm lips, the warming of his eyes to pure gold, the softening of his features. "We'll have to leave early from Shinjuku. Can you be ready by 6:00 a.m.?"

"I'll be ready."

Randy hung up the phone and eyed it for a moment. Not for a second did she suppose that Ken Sawa had asked her to go with him out of the kindness of his heart. The man had a devious motive, but forewarned was forearmed. Manipulation was like hypnosis. It only worked with the victim's consent.

Randy repeated this thought like a mantra next morning when Sawa Industries's sleek sedan picked her up at the hotel and drove her and Ken into Tokyo to catch the bullet train. She was on her guard at first, but Ken seemed relaxed and friendly, and as the sleek, modern train flashed on its way, pointed out that town followed town and city with hardly any interruption.

"At one time there'd have been farmlands and rice paddies between towns," he told her. "They'd be emerald green at this time of year."

"And all that beauty has gone in the name of progress. Is that what you're saying?"

He smiled at the provocative note in her voice. "Japan's a small country, Randy. People have to live somewhere. Besides, back in the days of open farms and paddies, trains took almost eight hours to get from Tokyo to Osaka. They weren't much better than the one to Gora."

The *shinkansen* arrived at its destination in little less than three hours. Randy had to agree, as they stepped onto Shin-Osaka Station, that the bullet train was far superior to its country cousin.

"Where to?" she asked as they walked out into a cool, overcast day. The sky was heavy with what looked like rain clouds, and she wished she'd added a raincoat to her gray suit and amber blouse.

"I have some business at the Regent Hotel," he replied. "It won't take too long."

Junjiro Sawa had built this handsome building back in the fifties. While Ken was concluding his business, Randy took photos outside and inside the lobby, which was cooled by a waterfall that flowed down one wall. The water from the falls splashed into a carp-filled pond and then was diverted into a shallow stream that drifted through the lobby.

The walls of this lobby were tastefully decorated with artwork, and Randy spent some time admiring them. She was especially interested in a framed photograph of a young man with a sensitive face and intelligent eyes.

"My father as a young man." She hadn't heard Ken's footfall across the plush carpet. "The Regent is one of his earlier buildings and one of his favorites. You'll see that he incorporated traditional Japanese features into a modern setting."

Though infinitely more grand and modern, the busy hotel managed to convey the tranquillity she'd found at the Inn of the Golden Bamboo. "Your father is a fine architect," Randy said sincerely.

"He's a man of vision." There was pride and affection in Ken's tone.

"I wish I could meet him," Randy said. "I'd very much like to know how he came by the idea for Sawa Town."

"Unfortunately he still hasn't yet recovered from that virus." Ken glanced at his watch. "Our train back to Tokyo leaves in a few hours, and you haven't done any sight-seeing yet. Good tourists always go to Osaka Castle. What about it?''

Randy decided to let Sawa Town go for now and bide her time. But as they took a taxi toward Osaka Castle, the image of the younger Junjiro stayed with her. What had changed that sensitive-looking young man to a shogun who cared little about historical and environmental issues?

Could he have been embittered by his wife's death? She wondered how she could bring up the subject as they arrived at Osaka Castle, which stood on a hill like a sentinel over the city. Ken slid an arm through Randy's as they walked up the path toward the castle gate.

''The first stones were laid back in 1853,'' Ken told her, ''and it took a hundred thousand workmen to build the walls. Those huge rocks you see were dredged out of the Inland Sea and hauled out here to become the base of the castle. They're older than the castle itself.''

She was having trouble concentrating on what he was saying. The arm through hers conveyed a low-voltage charge that seeped through her blouse and skin and into her veins. As they walked, her thigh touched his, and the contact was even more disturbing. Under the pretext of taking out her camera, Randy freed her arm and took a few steps away.

''The castle itself was burned down in 1868 when the Tokugawa shogunate crumbled,'' Ken was telling her. ''This one was rebuilt in 1931. It's marginally smaller than the original version, but an exact replica otherwise and much more durable. There's an elevator inside, too, which makes climbing to the eighth floor a lot easier."

Randy began to laugh. "You've tipped your hand, mister. Even in castles, you feel that modern is better."

He pretended to look hurt. "All I'm doing is helping you do your duty as a tourist."

For the next half hour they roamed the castle, pausing at its museum and ending up on its observation deck on the eighth floor. Then Ken said, "Well, now that you've fulfilled your *giri,* it's time to have fun."

"Ninjo," she said quickly.

His smile made him look young and carefree. "Right. What would you like to do for fun, Randy?"

The cloudy day threw shadows that emphasized his strong jaw and the curve of his lips. Randy could remember the texture, the taste of that mouth, and there was a tingle in her fingertips—almost a need—to run her hands through his dark, wind-ruffled hair.

"What would you enjoy?" Ken murmured.

Randy tried to talk around the lump that had formed in her throat. It wouldn't budge. She gulped hard and heard herself mutter, "How about lunch?"

Food was the farthest thing from Ken's mind. He discovered that he'd been holding his breath as he focused on Randy's upturned face. Even under these sunless skies, her eyes were emerald, and he'd missed her subtle scent. They were standing so close that if either of them moved a step, they would end up in each other's arms.

It was high time he got himself in hand. "Lunch," Ken agreed in a hearty voice. "A great idea. Playing tourist always makes me hungry."

A somewhat harrowing taxi ride back to town re-established their equilibrium. Half an hour later Randy was staring about her at a bewildering array of eateries, bars, nightclubs and brightly lit stores where men and women were playing pinball machines. She'd read that *pachinko* was the national pastime and that even members of the Diet relaxed this way.

"Just where are we?" she wondered.

"In the heart of Osaka's pleasure area. People come here to have fun." Ken slid an arm through Randy's and led her across the street.

Looking around her, Randy said, "Duty and pleasure. In a way, that's at the heart of this conflict about Sawa Town."

"You've lost me there."

Though he hadn't moved a muscle, she sensed his renewed tension. "Your father wants to build Sawa Town for his pleasure," Randy pointed out, "but other people feel he has a duty not to do so."

"Don't try to analyze what you don't understand, Randy."

The pleasant, laid-back companion of the day had gone. Ken's eyes were hard, the line of his mouth arrogantly tight. This was the other side of Ken Sawa, the flip side of the coin. Randy felt a small spasm of regret before the reporter in her took charge.

"Then perhaps you can explain it to me so that I *can* understand," she said.

If only I could—

The thought came out of nowhere and hit Ken with disturbing force. Before he could deal with it, Randy put a hand to her cheek. "It's raining," she exclaimed.

As if her words were some kind of signal, the heavens opened up, and raindrops the size of marbles descended from the heavy gray sky. Ken grabbed Randy's hand and began to run for the nearest building.

They reached it just as there was a long, angry peal of thunder. "It's only a passing shower," Ken said. "We'll wait it out in here."

Glass doors sighed open in front of them, and Randy followed Ken into a foyer made luxurious by a plush, crimson carpet and deep red armchairs. Ornately framed portraits hung on the walls.

Apparently they were in a hotel, for there was a reception area to one side. There was also a bar near the elevators.

A young man in tuxedo and black tie came forward from behind the reception area and bowed obsequiously. "Honored guests," he murmured. "Welcome."

As he spoke, a young and well-dressed couple rose from the bar and walked toward the elevators. "We're not staying," Randy explained. "We've only taken refuge from the rain."

The clerk bowed again. "Yes, madam," he said in careful English, "of course. Perhaps you would care for a drink while waiting for the weather to change?"

Randy glanced at Ken, who said, "A glass of wine?"

It would be impolite to use the hotel as shelter without buying so much as a drink. Randy nodded and thought she saw a sly smile flicker for a moment on the clerk's lips a second before he bowed and retreated.

She asked for a club soda with a twist of lime and looked about her. It was then that she realized that the portraits that hung on the walls were all of nude women. "What's the name of this hotel?" she asked as Ken returned with their drinks.

"I believe it's called the Sumire."

Thinking that "the violet" was an odd name for a hotel, Randy nevertheless sat down and returned to their earlier discussion. "Ken," she said, "we didn't finish talking about Sawa Town. If I offended you, I'm sorry. It's just that though you've told me how you stand, you haven't explained why the hurry to get Sawa Town built."

Wordlessly he leaned back in his armchair and crossed his long legs. Realizing that he was using silence as a tactic to unnerve her, Randy continued, "At least, it seems to me as though you are in a hurry. Otherwise, why push Sawa Town down so many people's throats when a little delay, a little diplomacy, could soothe ruffled feathers?"

The dull red of the armchair in which she was sitting was a foil for her silver-gray suit and the dark fall of her hair. Randy looked lovely sitting there, Ken thought. The trouble was that she was also too intelligent for anyone's good.

"There's more at stake than you realize," he began.

"Time costs money," she agreed. "I understand that. But surely goodwill is more important than profit margins? Roughly half of the people I interviewed in Asatsuki were critical of your smashing down Yui Hill."

"Tell me about them."

"Well, there was Mr. Murai. He said he'd sailed kites from the top of the hill as a boy and hated to think that he couldn't take his grandsons there. And there were so many others. The place has a sense of tradition, Ken."

He didn't say anything, just sat there sipping his drink. His face gave away none of his thoughts or emotions. Randy decided to try a new tack.

"Yui Hill reminds me of Bullfrog Creek," she said.

"Who or what is Bullfrog Creek?"

He sounded polite but bored. It reminded Randy of how he'd acted that day of their first meeting. Ken was building a wall around himself and she needed to tear it down.

"Bullfrog Creek," she said in a deceptively hearty voice, "was where my brothers used to go to catch the biggest frogs come Frog Leaping Day at Meldon's county fair. They used to win the frog races every time because they knew just where to go."

In spite of himself, Ken felt himself start to grin. "What happened to the frogs later? Did they end up as bill of fare in some French restaurant?"

"Perish the thought. They were returned to Bullfrog Creek with honors. Dad used to say that Pete and Charlie got the same frogs every year. It's sad that they won't be able to take their sons there because the creek was dammed up back in '81 to make room for a high-way.''

As Randy told her story, she'd noticed that several couples had come strolling down the crimson-carpeted stairs to the left. Others entered the hotel, had a drink at the bar and then walked to the elevators. A suspicion began to form in her mind, and she finally asked, ''What kind of place *is* this?''

''They call it a 'love hotel,''' he replied.

''A *what?*''

''It's not a house of ill repute, if that's what you're thinking. The Sumire is a respectable establishment that caters to the fantasies of its clients.''

The clerk now sidled out of the reception area and came to stand behind Ken. He whispered something. ''What did he say?'' Randy demanded.

''He wanted to know if we'd like to look over the rooms and make our selection.''

''Is it possible to just *look?*'' she asked cautiously.

''Are you sure you want to expose yourself to temptation?''

His half smile held a challenge, and she threw it back at him. ''Hey, it's not every day that a girl gets to check out a 'love hotel.'''

A flick of the clerk's finger summoned a woman attendant, who accompanied them up the elevator to the second floor. Here she unlocked a door and stepped back. ''After you,'' Ken said.

Randy walked into the room and blinked, for the chamber had been designed to look like a jungle. Large potted palms stood against walls festooned with moss and vines. Parrots and other exotic birds screeched from cages suspended from the ceiling. Chairs and tables, fashioned out of fake zebra and leopard skins, flanked an enormous circular bed. A canopy of vines curtained the bed.

"Who sleeps here, Tarzan?" she gasped.

"Maybe that chimpanzee of his," Ken suggested.

There was a muted roar, followed immediately by jungle drums. Randy jumped, then realized that their guide had flipped on a stereo. As sounds of the jungle closed in about them, Ken said, "I take it that we don't want this room."

"Not unless a stampede of wild elephants turns you on." Randy shook her head as they left the room. "You mean people really sleep there?"

"I doubt if they get much sleep," Ken said.

Ignoring the implication in his voice, Randy followed their guide to the Moulin Rouge Room, which resembled a French bordello. Randy had never seen a bordello, but she could imagine that the rooms of such an establishment would be decorated in various shades of red, with accents that were heavy on black lace. The heart-shaped bed was swatched in layers of crimson satin and curtained with scarlet velvet drapes.

"Does it excite you unbearably?" Ken asked as the stereo began to play "La Vie en Rose."

"Not unless claustrophobia is a turn-on."

They'd spoken in English, but even so, their guide seemed slightly miffed. "We have many honeymoon couples who ask for the Moulin Rouge," she volunteered.

Randy wondered, "Do couples come here on their *honeymoon?*"

"Some people need all the help they can get."

Ken's voice was unsteady. Randy said, "I think I've had about as much *ninjo* as I can take for one afternoon. Can we leave?"

"You'll hurt our guide's feelings if you don't let her give us the grand tour," Ken pointed out. "She's got to earn her tip."

Some of the rooms were, in their guide's polite words, temporarily occupied. The ones she showed them included a bird room, an underwater fantasy chamber and a carousel room, complete with a full-size carousel that had been placed near the bed. "For diversion or perversion?" Ken whispered wickedly. "The up-down motion of the carousel must be powerful stuff. What's the next attraction?"

It was called the Maiden's Retreat. Randy, prepared for almost anything, found this room to be a pleasant surprise. After the garish sensuality she'd seen, the Maiden's Retreat seemed as wholesome as sunshine. The walls and curtains were all in white, the carpet was white with a sprinkling of flowers and the lace-canopied bed looked delicate and inviting. Then a second look told her that the chamber was subtly sensual. The low table set with fruit and two wine glasses, the flower petals that had been sprinkled on the turned-down sheets—all whispered an invitation.

Sunlight and flowers and Randy— The errant thought accompanied a stab of wholly inappropriate desire and caught Ken unprepared. His mind was invaded with images that made him gasp aloud—a sound he turned to a cough at the last moment.

Was he catching cold in this cool place? Randy glanced up at him, which was a mistake. In the heart's beat of time before she could drag her eyes away, she envisioned herself lying in Ken's arms. The press of his bare chest would be hard against her breasts, the flower petals cool against her naked back.

Randy gulped hard, tried to speak, and could only swallow again. "Don't we have a train to catch?" she finally managed to say.

Ken didn't trust himself to speak. One moment the Sumire had been amusing, but now he didn't feel like laughing. All he really wanted to do was tear Randy's clothes off her and carry her to that waiting bed.

Giving their guide her tip, they escaped outside. The sky was still lowering, but the rain had ceased and the air was fresh. Randy drew a deep breath as Ken commented, "Well, you did want to see it."

She nodded. "It was—interesting."

"But?"

"The Inn of the Golden Bamboo wins hands down."

And of course she was right. Randy Muir didn't need special effects to make her desirable, Ken thought—all she needed was to be herself.

"For once I have to agree with you," he said.

She pretended to do a double-take. "Can I quote you on that? 'Ken Sawa agrees that the glitzy and the new doesn't hold a candle to the old and traditional.' There. Did I get it right?"

"Anyone ever tell you that you talk too much?"

Chapter Five

"It is seven o'clock in the night," Minako protested. "Have you partaken of dinner, Ran-dee?"

Randy glanced at a stale sandwich lying half-hidden on her rumpled desk. "I'd forgotten about eating," she confessed. "Why are you here, anyway? I thought you had test papers to grade."

"Shin-san wanted to see you," Minako explained. "The historical environmentalist movement needs your help, Ran-dee."

Randy's stomach gave a low, protesting growl. "Lead me to food first," she pleaded. Then she added, "So you and the secretary of the society are now on a first-name basis?"

Minako's cheeks turned a delicate pink. "We have decided not to be ceremonious. After all, we are working together to save Yui Hill."

Shin Naka was waiting in the hotel lobby. He was wearing a dark suit that made him look thinner than ever, and his eyes behind the thick glasses gleamed with a martial fire as he bowed to Randy. After a whispered conference, he and Minako led the way to a small eatery behind the hotel, a place that served delicious-looking griddle cakes heaped with a choice of condiments.

"We call this *okonomiyaki*—literally, 'fried to your taste,'" Minako explained. "Try the seafood pancake, Ran-dee. It has kelp in it. Kelp is very nutritious."

The kelp was chewy and had an interesting but not unpleasant taste that blended well with the delectable sauces, crab and shrimps that were heaped onto the pancake. Between bites of her *okonomiyaki* and sips of Japanese beer, Randy managed to ask, "Did you have your meeting with Ken Sawa yet?"

Shin looked frustrated. "He keeps putting us off. That devious man is waiting for interest in our movement to die down."

"I heard that he went to Ashiya yesterday to see his father." Minako switched to English so that Randy was sure to understand as she added, "We are fearing that he will bring back the order to start demolishing Yui Hill. Ran-dee, please help us come up with an idea to keep the Sawas uncomfortable."

Randy promised to do some thinking, and Shin spent the evening entertaining her with stories and legends about Yoshitsune and Lady Shizuka. Fired with some of his enthusiasm, Randy went back to work and wrote half the night before weariness forced her to stop. It seemed she'd been asleep less than a few moments before the phone's shrill clamor woke her. She fumbled for the receiver blindly and heard a deep voice say, "Good morning, Randy."

Randy opened her eyes and winced as a flood of sunshine assailed her. She'd forgotten to draw the drapes before falling into bed last night. "What time is it?" she croaked.

"Six o'clock. You sound as if you're still in bed."

"I am. You should be, too," she muttered ungraciously.

"Is that an invitation?" The intimate note in his voice conjured up an image of his powerful body lying next to her among the rumpled sheets. She could see the darkness of his hair against the white pillow and breathe in his clean, vibrant scent.

Randy sat bolt upright in bed. "Why are you calling me?" she demanded.

"To ask if you want to go to Kyoto," he replied.

Didn't the man ever get tired? He'd just traveled to Ashiya. Before that, there'd been the trip to Osaka, and the one to Hakone. Randy tried to cudgel her sleep-impaired brain back into operation. "Why Kyoto?" she asked.

"There's a man you might want to meet," Ken said. "He's a sword maker who still practices that centuries-old art. Interested?"

Wide awake suddenly, Randy slid her legs over the side of the bed. "You bet I am."

"I thought so." She was so excited about the prospect of meeting a master craftsman that she didn't even resent his smug tone. "Umezono-*sensei* is descended from five generations of sword makers."

Randy's cloud of euphoria thinned enough to admit suspicion. Up until now Ken had been doing his best to convince her—and *Issues Today*—that new was better. Now, all of a sudden, he was pushing the ancient art of sword making.

"Wait a minute," Randy said. "Back up, here. Just why are you doing this for me?"

Instead of answering, he asked, "Can you be ready in an hour, or am I asking the impossible?"

So he wasn't going to tell her. She'd have to play along and see what happened. "Are you kidding?" Randy exclaimed. "I'll be ready in half that time."

It took less than twenty minutes to shower the last vestiges of sleep away and select a dress of slubbed raw silk with a hint of green in the matching jacket. By the time Ken came strolling through the door of the Asatsuki Grand Hotel, Randy was drinking her second cup of coffee.

She'd thought he would be dressed formally for the occasion, but he was wearing a blazer tossed carelessly over a sport shirt and informal slacks. "Umezono-*sensei* isn't the kind of man to stand on ceremony," he explained.

"You know him well?"

"I was good friends with his second son, Tosa." As Ken spoke his eyes roved approvingly over her. "Charming," he said. "You look like springtime."

And *he* looked like the tomcat who was about to swallow the canary. Not *this* bird, Randy thought grimly. "How was your trip to Ashiya?" she asked. "Is your father feeling better?"

How had she known about Ashiya? Ken wondered. He looked down into Randy's luminous green eyes and wondered what she would do if he told her the plain, unadorned truth. For a moment he was tempted to do just that, but sanity returned in time.

"You know how stubborn viruses can be, but he's making progress." He motioned to the door. "Shall we?"

He didn't want to discuss his father. It was a bad sign. Perhaps Minny was right and Junjiro had ordered the destruction of Yui Hill. "Have any decisions been made?" she asked casually.

"None that need concern us today," was his equally offhanded reply. "Do you know anything about the art of sword making?"

Apparently *he* knew a great deal, and by the time he'd finished, they were back on the *shinkansen* and riding toward Kyoto. "How did you learn all that?" Randy asked, impressed.

"Like many Japanese boys, I was taught kendo, the art of sword fighting, when I was young," he replied. "I used to have a wooden sword, a costume, a face guard, the whole nine yards. In the evenings, after my lesson, I would give my parents a demonstration of my progress."

"It sounds like fun."

"It was."

"What else did you do?" she asked.

"Since my father believed that English was the language of business, I was sent to Japanese school in the morning and English classes in the afternoon. Whenever I could get away from my studies, I played sports. There were family vacations." Ken shrugged. "How about you, growing up in the cornfields of Kansas?"

"I had a nice, safe, boring childhood," she replied. "My brothers and sisters and I went to school, played, got into the usual kinds of trouble."

There was a look in his eyes that was hard to read. It wasn't sadness, really—more like regret. But it was gone instantly, before she could analyze it. "Tell me more," he said cheerfully.

She'd wanted to concentrate on him, to draw out more of his childhood reminiscences. She had forgotten with whom she was dealing. In the little more than two hours they took to reach Kyoto, Ken had gotten her to tell him pretty much everything there was to know about the Muirs. She'd even told him about her great-grandpa Cotton Muir, who'd come west in a covered wagon and who'd disgraced the family by getting roaring drunk while Great-grandma was entertaining the church ladies' sewing society.

"It wasn't funny," she added when Ken laughed. "Great-grandma swore she'd leave him right then and there."

"Did she?"

"Nope. The sneaky old buzzard talked himself into her good graces before she'd even started to pack. I'm told Great-grandpa was the kind of man who could convince you black was really pink. He was the greatest manipulator since . . . Houdini."

That wasn't the name she'd meant to say, Ken knew. Instinct told him that something had happened to

Randy Muir, something that could still dull the luster of her eyes. He also intuited that her trouble had something to do with a man.

A man had left her with those shadows, those bruises in her eyes. Ken realized that he'd clenched his hands into fists. He wanted to fight the man who had hurt Randy and shake him till his teeth rattled. He wanted to knock him down. Such primitive, barbaric emotions were not like him, and Ken was both astonished at himself and wary. He couldn't afford to allow this green-eyed woman to get to him in this way.

Of course, he'd been under a lot of pressure lately, and pressure affected people differently. Ken drew a deep mental breath and willed himself to listen to Randy, who was asking a question about Kyoto's history and culture.

The farthest thing from Randy's mind was history and culture, but she needed time to pull herself together. She couldn't believe that she'd almost told Ken about Nate Brady.

Her lapse of good judgment was something she couldn't even begin to understand, but then her reactions to Ken were completely insane. One moment his smug attitude made her want to kick him, and the next minute she was ready to tell him her deepest secrets.

Randy reminded herself that she was dealing with Junjiro Sawa's son. Charming though the man was, the cool blood of the "shogun of modern industry" ran in his veins, and he would try and twist her to his own ends. Right now his ends were to convince her that the destruction of Yui Hill was justified.

She was lost in these thoughts when the bullet train slid into Kyoto Station. Almost immediately Randy was struck with an incongruity. In the midst of the bustling, cosmopolitan city, a huge five-tiered pagoda rose like a giant from another age.

The sword maker's workshop was another surprise. Randy had expected Umezono-*sensei*'s workshop to be in some tranquil and unspoiled part of Kyoto. She was astonished when the taxi took them to an alley off a busy thoroughfare.

"The door's never locked," Ken said, opening the gate and ushering Randy into the compound. On one side was a small house, and on the other a spacious workshop. A garden lay between the two.

"Do I disturb?" Ken called.

A young man came hurrying out of the workshop in answer to Ken's call. "Kenjiro!" he exclaimed. "Ever since your phone call, the family's talked of nothing but your visit. Welcome to this house."

"It's good to see you again, Tosa!"

The men shook hands in the Western way, slapping each other's shoulders. As they grinned at each other, Randy saw that though the swordsmith's son was shorter than Ken, he had the powerful build and alert look of a trained athlete. He bowed as Ken introduced him to Randy and said, "Excuse my poor English, Randy-san. I am very glad to meet you. Please come inside to meet my father."

"Thank you, and you speak English very well," Randy said. The young man actually blushed.

"Oh, no, oh, no, very poor," he stammered. "I do not practice enough. I have a very bad head for languages."

"Actually he's a fair linguist," Ken commented as the other man went into the house. "Besides English, he speaks French and Chinese."

Randy looked puzzled. "I've noticed that Japanese people don't know what to do with compliments," she remarked. "Minny's the same. Why is that?"

"Japanese believe that accepting compliments makes them appear conceited and self-centered."

As Ken spoke, they came into the center of the workshop. Here, a serious-looking man, older than Tosa, was firing a forge. A tall, gray-haired man, so thin as to be almost gaunt, was seated beside the forge. He was dressed in a loose white robe and wore a small, black-lacquered hat on his head. He was heating what looked to be a narrow block of steel in the forge.

"*Sensei,* I'm honored to see you again," Ken said.

There was a note of unfeigned respect in Ken's voice, and his bow was low. The old man looked up, nodded cheerfully and said, "Not at all, Kenjiro. It is good to see you after so long a time."

His voice was soft, and he had a sweet smile. "You have come to watch me at my work?" the swordsmith continued.

"Yes, and as I told you over the phone, I've brought an American lady to meet you," Ken said. "This is Randy Muir. She's writing an article on the traditions of Japan."

The gray-haired man included Randy in his smile and nodded a welcome. Pointing to the second young man he said, "This is my son and apprentice, Kinmatsu. He and I are about to flatten the steel. Tosa has come to watch us this morning, and the two of you may watch also."

A respectful silence fell over the workshop as the old man once more concentrated on the steel. "The metal must be the exact color of the sunset," he muttered, "or the blade will be useless. The sword that is being forged here must have purity as well as strength."

Suddenly he withdrew the steel from the flames. "Now!" he commanded.

He laid the steel on an anvil, and his son began to pound it with a heavy sledgehammer. "The blade must be flattened," Umezono-*sensei* continued in an absorbed voice. "Then it is folded lengthwise and then flattened again. Over and over this is done. In this way the fused layers will have strength and flexibility."

After a few minutes Ken touched Randy's shoulder. "I think that the *sensei* needs to work in peace. Let's go into the garden."

They walked out into the garden, which was not a formal Japanese garden but a homey place with a vegetable patch, budding peach trees and morning-glory vines. There was also a muddy frog-pond edged with Japanese iris.

Randy's mind was still on what she had seen in the workshop. "How hot does that forge get?" Randy wanted to know.

"Upward of two thousand degrees Fahrenheit," Ken replied. "That's pretty hot."

"I'll say it is. How does the *sensei* measure the temperature?"

"As he does everything else—by eye, instinct and timing. It's the old way."

She couldn't resist. "So you do admit that tradition has its value."

"Life would be meaningless without tradition," he replied. "But tradition has its place. If old and new can't coexist, the law of nature takes over. Be careful here. The ground's not even."

As if it were the most natural thing in the world, he slid an arm through hers and drew her hard against his side. For a moment Randy was acutely conscious of the hard, lean strength of him pressed against her, but she forced herself to concentrate on what Ken had just said.

"Supposing that a modern thoroughfare had to be built in Kyoto and cut right through the *sensei*'s workshop," she asked. "Would you say that that was the law of nature?"

Her voice was husky with challenge, and Ken frowned. For a moment, here in the tranquil garden, he had forgotten about their differences. Impatient words rose to his lips, but he stopped them in time. He hadn't brought Randy here to quarrel with her.

Carefully Ken voiced words of calm reason. "The *sensei,* being a man of sense, would relocate."

"Why couldn't the road go around his workshop?"

"The city engineers could probably give you a few good reasons. Anyway, we're discussing a hypothetical case."

Randy noted that Ken's expression was turning obstinate. "There are certain things that can't be moved," she pointed out.

"Like that moss, I suppose," he growled.

They were standing inches apart, and as usual his size was intimidating. Randy forced herself to stand her ground and not to take a cowardly step backward. "It's not *my* moss. Yoshitsune's Tears belong to the world." Had he snorted? she wondered wrathfully. Maybe she'd been a tad melodramatic there, but Ken could bring out the worst in her. At times he reminded her of her brother Pete, who'd goad her and goad her until she'd lose her temper and try to beat him up. Only, Ken was in no way, shape or form like Pete.

Coldly she said, "You *are* aware that if you destroy Yui Hill, you'll destroy not only Yoshitsune's Rock but a rare life-form."

"You make it sound like murder."

"You said it, not me."

His eyes narrowed. His nostrils flared. He looked like a bull about to charge. "The moss is useless. It does no good to anyone. Besides, what happened to your claim that you were impartial?"

With deadly calm Randy retorted, "I'm merely clarifying your stand for the record. May I quote what you just said? You said, 'The moss is useless'—"

Before she could continue, there were voices at the door of the workshop and the *sensei,* followed by his sons, strode out.

"In order to work well, spirit and body must both be nourished," the *sensei* called cheerfully. "It is now time for the body."

"My father means that it's lunchtime," Tosa explained. "Naturally you'll join us?"

"I thought you'd never ask."

Not looking at Randy, Ken fell into step with Tosa. Randy followed in a seething silence that lasted until they had reached the house. Here Umezono called, "Okitsu, our guests have arrived."

A pleasant-faced middle-aged lady came hurrying out to kneel on the raised upper step. She clapped her hands when she saw Ken and exclaimed, "Welcome, welcome, Kenjiro-san. My goodness! It has been such a long time since we saw you last."

"Kenjiro has brought a lady writer from America," Umezono-*sensei* explained, and Randy was swiftly included in the lady's welcome.

"Come on, come in. It is a small, shabby place, but please enter," Mrs. Umezono insisted. "Hisako-san and I will bring the food at once."

Though the little house was furnished entirely in the Japanese manner with golden tatami floors and little furniture, Randy noted modern conveniences. There was an air-conditioning unit, a large television set, and as she passed the open doorway to the tiny kitchen she saw a stove, refrigerator and microwave all in harvest gold.

Umezono himself ushered them into a room that fronted the garden. As he insisted that Ken take the seat of honor, Randy noted the sword that lay before the scroll.

She had no time for more than a swift glance, for the rest of the family was now introduced. Hisako, Kinmatsu's wife, was a round-faced, merry-eyed young woman, and her daughter Chii-chan was about five years old. With her sleek, bowl-cut black hair and big black eyes set in a smooth, olive face, Chii-chan was like a tiny doll.

After a shy peep at Randy, she danced over to her grandfather, plopped into his lap and announced, "I have been waiting and *waiting* for lunch, Grandpa. You and daddy and Uncle Tosa worked too long, as usual."

"Well, you won't have to wait any longer," her mother announced as she helped her mother-in-law bring in trays of food. "Please—" she dimpled at Randy "—our food is very plain and badly cooked, but we would be honored if you taste it."

As she ate, Randy watched Ken's interaction with the *sensei* and his sons. He seemed genuinely happy to be with his friends. This quintessentially modern man seemed at home in this traditional setting.

But Hisako did not give Randy time to pursue her thoughts. She was curious about America and even more curious about the role of women in the States. She herself held a job as manager of quality control at a large textile firm in Kyoto, she said, but had taken a holiday in honor of Ken and his guest.

Randy was intrigued. She knew that a Japanese woman of good family hardly ever worked outside the home after she had children. "Have you held the position long?" she asked.

The young woman nodded. "I worked at it before I was married and afterward, too. When Chii-chan was born, Kinmatsu and I discussed whether I should leave my job. Luckily my husband is a feminist."

At the look of inquiry in Randy's eyes, Hisako hurried to explain.

"He is respectful and helpful toward women. Not all Japanese men are like that, so I am very lucky. Because Kinmatsu is a *feministo,* he spoke up for me to the family, and it was decided that after Chii-chan entered school, I might return to work. Kinmatsu understands that I love my job almost as much as he loves sword making."

Automatically Randy glanced at the sword.

"No, that sword is not of my making," the *sensei* said, answering her unspoken question. "My great-grandfather made it for a samurai of the Tokugawa shogunate. The samurai died before he could claim his sword, and his family returned it to Great-grandfather. Tosa, let me have the sword."

When the young man had done as he asked, Umezono unsheathed it. Light danced across the blade, dazzling Randy with its silvery sheen. With a ceremonial bow, the old swordsmith grasped the sword in both hands and extended it to Randy. Conscious that a great honor was being conferred on her, she accepted the weapon.

"Samurai believed that they could not use a weapon such as this unless they had a pure heart," the *sensei* explained. "The best samurai were scholars, as well as great swordsmen. Many were poets, like Yoshitsune.

I often thought that if Ken Sawa had been born in another age, he would have been a great samurai.''

Ken bowed. "You flatter me.''

"You were always a bright boy, and you had the soul of a poet. As for your sword arm, you used to be a match for Tosa. However, these days Tosa is a teacher of kendo and has his own school.''

Tosa's eyes gleamed. "Would you like a match, Kenjiro? For old time's sake?''

"Did you have to ask me *after* I stuffed myself on your mother's cooking?'' Ken laughed, but the others insisted and Chii-chan clapped her hands.

"Please, Uncle Kenjiro,'' she cried. "It will be so exciting for you to fight Uncle Tosa. It will be like a samurai movie where the hero kills all his enemies.''

"Bloodthirsty brat.'' Ken laughed as he gave in.

Chii-chan looked delighted, and Tosa said, "Come with me and we'll get you outfitted. I promise to go easy on you.''

Ken saw Randy frown and leaned forward to whisper, "Worried about me?''

"Well, sort of. I'd never find my way back to Asatsuki without you.''

"They'll call you a taxi.'' Ken swung to his feet and left the room with Tosa. Mrs. Umezono clicked her tongue.

"Men never grow up,'' she declared. "Randy-san, do you know that Kenjiro-san and Tosa spent their summers together in Hakone? They were always falling out of trees and fencing with bamboo poles.''

The images made Randy smile. Mrs. Umezono continued, "Kenjiro-san's father once commissioned my husband for a sword and they became friends. Our sons knew each other when they were young, and they took kendo lessons together during the summers.'' Mrs. Umezono paused. "After his mother's death, Kenjiro-san came to visit us often. He was so lonely, the poor boy. Now he has grown into such a handsome man and has accomplished wonderful things. We are all so proud of him.''

Randy hesitated for a second, then decided to ask, "Have you heard about Sawa Town?'' The elderly lady nodded. "What do you think of the controversy that surrounds Yui Hill?''

The older woman looked calmly at Randy. "Kenjiro-san must have his reasons.''

Randy didn't know what to say to that, so she remained silent. "Some people find it easy to destroy things,'' Mrs. Umezono went on. "Kenjiro-san is too intelligent for that. So if he is destroying something as important as a hill, he must have a good reason.''

Just then Tosa and Ken came into the garden. The men had replaced their shoes with straw sandals and discarded their modern clothes for white shirts and long, loose black trousers that flowed from a fitted waist to a wide base at the ankle. Randy thought that the costume suited Ken. With his proud carriage and confident tilt of head, he had the look of his samurai ancestors.

The two men were carrying long wooden swords and had metal visors tucked under their arms. Though they were talking and laughing as they came up to the porch, they became grave as, kneeling on the ground, they bowed to the *sensei*.

"We are here to engage in combat," Tosa said formally. "We look to you for guidance, my father."

"Be honorable and do your best," was the equally formal reply.

Randy found that she was holding her breath as Ken and Tosa got to their feet and snapped on their visors. They faced each other and bowed deeply. Then, stepping back, they raised their wooden swords. With all the ritual of a ceremonial dance, the swords were arched back. Then, with a shout, Tosa leapt forward to strike.

Randy stifled a cry, but Ken easily parried Tosa's blow. She watched in fascination as the two combatants now circled each other, exchanging blows and parries. Each movement, each step and flex of arm or wrist, had meaning, Randy saw. She also noted that Ken was in control of every nerve and that his instincts were all honed to one purpose—to win.

And she *wanted* him to win. Randy realized that she was almost as tense as Ken. Her hands were clasped so tightly in her lap that her nails dug into her palms, and she gasped when Ken sprang to the attack. As his practiced thrust sent Tosa's weapon flying, she couldn't keep back a cry of approval.

Tosa lunged after his weapon, but Ken put his foot on it. Next moment, he had the point of his wooden sword at Tosa's throat. "The match goes to Kenjiro," Umezono-*sensei* cried.

Tosa acknowledged his defeat good-humoredly. "You've been practicing," he accused.

"You took pity on me and let me win," Ken replied courteously.

He drew off his visor as he spoke, and met Randy's eyes. The look in them hit him harder than any of Tosa's blows. Randy's eyes were swimming with emerald light, and her cheeks were flushed.

She looked lovelier than he'd ever seen her, and when she smiled at him, he felt something turn inside his heart. Ken didn't understand the emotion he was experiencing, but he knew that this feeling went far deeper than mere triumph. If they'd been alone, he'd have been tempted to take Randy into his arms.

Walking over to her, he affected a casual tone. "Didn't think I could do it, did you?"

With her usual honesty, she shook her head. "Tosa teaches kendo. Even so, when you squared up to each other, I sort of hoped—"

She didn't finish the sentence, and she didn't have to. Her eyes were shining as she smiled up at him, and for a moment they seemed totally connected with each other. A sense of partnership and understanding that needed no words bridged the narrow physical space between them.

The urge to kiss her, hold her, do *something*, was too strong to ignore. Hardly realizing that he was doing so, Ken picked a flower that grew by the veranda. "Thanks for being my cheering section," he said.

As he tucked the flower in her hair, Randy remembered that long ago a victorious knight offered his lady-love a crown of flowers. The cheerful talk around her and the sun-warmed garden all dimmed until only she and Ken were real. Nothing existed in this suddenly breathless place but the scent of the flower Ken had picked for her, the touch of his long fingers brushing her cheek.

Something went very still in Randy's heart. It was as if she were waiting for something incredible to happen. But nothing did happen. Instead, Ken nodded casually to her and strolled off to talk with Tosa.

Randy listened to Ken laughing and comparing notes about other matches. Impatiently she shook her mind free of foolishness and moonshine. She reminded herself that this was modern-day Japan, not the days of chivalry. And if Ken Sawa was a knight in shining armor, she was the Queen of May.

Chapter Six

The visit to the Umezonos lingered late into the afternoon. Ken and Tosa relived their younger days over bottles of Japanese beer, and the old master brought out more of his precious swords to show Randy. When they finally left, Hisako hugged Randy.

"I must now say *sayonara,* which means, 'if it must be so,'" she explained. "Please come again, Randy-san."

Randy hated to go. "What a wonderful family," she told Ken when they were strolling down the alley toward the main road. "It's incredible how Umezono-*sensei* has preserved traditions."

"Actually the Umezonos have a modern outlook," Ken pointed out. "A traditional family wouldn't have allowed Hisako-san to go back to her job."

"Supposing the family decided that Hisako-san shouldn't work," Randy wondered. "Do you think she would have put up a fight?"

"It's highly unlikely."

"But surely *her* wishes count for something," Randy was beginning when her eye caught a small roadside shrine. "That's in honor of Ojizo-san, isn't it?"

Paper pinwheels decorated the ground around a benevolent, shaven-headed figure dressed in flowing robes. Someone had placed a red hat on the statue's head, and a scarf was wound around its neck. There were flowers before the shrine, as well as offerings of food: rice cakes, a handful of sweets, oranges and a chocolate bar.

Randy had seen photos, of course, but the reality was more poignant. These gifts weren't for Ojizo-san, who guided the souls of dead children to heaven. Randy felt a lump grow in her throat as she thought of the mother who had made that scarf and hat to keep her baby warm.

"The shrine helps women deal with their loss," Ken said quietly.

Randy touched the tip of a bright pinwheel and made it whirl. "I know. In a way, it reminds me of an article I wrote about a Japanese toy-maker who made some expensive, life-style dolls."

"For rich kids?"

She shook her head. "Would you believe that his clients were mostly old people? Their families had moved away, and the dolls became surrogate grandchildren. The old folks dealt with their loneliness by taking the dolls on walks, reading to them and so on.''

Ken looked somber. ''The family structure is breaking down because young people have to leave their hometowns to look for jobs. It's one aspect of the 'new' Japan that isn't too pleasant.''

''At least Sawa Industries is subsidizing places like Happiness,'' Randy pointed out.

''Perhaps that's because we know what happens when a family falls apart.''

His voice held a note she'd never heard before, and she looked up at him in surprise. ''I was nine when my mother died,'' Ken added.

They'd stopped walking. Somewhere in the quiet alleyway a child was playing a game, and the sing-song of its voice was like a thread dancing and weaving through Ken's deep tones as he continued, ''She was an aviator, a good one. She told me once that she never felt so free as when she was up in her plane. She was flying near the Japanese Alps when her plane's engine failed.'' He paused, and she could see his throat work around a swallow. ''She could have landed in a village. If she had, she might have managed to survive—but people would have been hurt. So she chose to come down in a forest. She and her plane went up in flames.''

He spoke without inflection, but Randy knew that each word exposed a raw nerve. She realized that she was holding her breath as he continued, ''When my father told me what happened, I was stunned. Then I got angry with her for dying and leaving me.''

Instinctively Randy sensed that Ken had not spoken of his mother's death to anyone before this. *Loss*, he had said, and for whatever reason, he was letting her see into his deepest wounds.

Wanting to comfort him, to erase the pain that he wouldn't allow to show in his words but which she could see in his eyes, Randy reached out and caught his hand in both of hers.

"I'm sorry," she whispered.

Ken's usually ordered mind was in a turmoil. He didn't know what had made him talk of events and emotions that he'd kept buried within himself for over twenty years. Why did I tell her? he wondered. Looking down into her upturned face, he discovered the answer.

Randy's eyes told him that she did more than understand and sympathize. She really wanted to take his pain away. Her mouth was soft, her underlip had a tremor to it, and he could no more stop himself from kissing her than he could stop breathing.

She knew that he was going to kiss her. She wanted him to. As Randy lifted her face to his, she felt as though she were a flower unfurling its petals to the sun. When his lips claimed hers, the warmth of that sun enveloped her completely.

Through a haze of sensations, she remembered the taste of his lips. Their texture. The rough-gentle rasp of his cheek against hers, the caressing magic of his hands in her hair. Then his hands roved down her back, tracing the curve of her spine, creating a trail of heat in their wake.

Her knees felt week, so she supported herself by wrapping her arms around him. Against her racing heart, she felt the uncompromising wall of his chest. Her stomach fitted against his lean belly, and the arrogant power of his thighs seemed to cradle her femininity.

Their lips stayed fused together. Unable to breathe, she opened her mouth and drew in oxygen from his lungs. Her tongue tip touched his, exploring, questing. An ache of longing, of need, of some thing undefinable but so strong as to be almost frightening, pulsed through her.

Ken felt Randy's heart pounding against his and felt as if the ground were rocking under his feet. The emotions he'd experienced while speaking of the past had brought the present moment into sharp focus. All his senses were alive to the woman in his arms. He couldn't get enough of the honey taste of Randy's mouth. He wanted to draw her scent into his lungs, to press her body closer to him until he lost himself in her.

Dropping one hand down her supple back to her hips, he pressed her even closer against him. Under the layers of fabric that separated them, he could feel the heat of her skin and could imagine the satin texture of it. The thought almost drove him mad.

The low, male growl he made deep in his throat stripped Randy of all lingering constraint. The primal sound went like an arrow to the depths of her need for this man. As he began to rain kisses on her face and throat, she knew she'd never felt like this before, not ever, not even with Nate.

She didn't want to think of Nate, not ever and especially not now, but his name caught hold of her mind and wouldn't let go. Like a burr, it irritated the surface of the bubble in which she was suspended, and a trickle of conscious thought returned.

Good grief, Randy thought. What am I doing?

What she was doing was standing in the street in broad daylight kissing Ken Sawa. What she was doing was acting like a crazy person. She could hear the sounds of traffic, a radio blaring nearby. And there were footsteps coming toward them—

Footsteps!

"S-someone's coming."

Her words followed Ken into the whirling vortex of his emotions. For a moment he ignored Randy's stammering warning, but then the footsteps echoed in his hazy brain like cannon fire.

He let go of Randy, moved a few steps away and blinked down into her face. Green eyes, dazed and a little scared, gazed back at him. What got into me? he wondered.

Seeing the shrine to Ojizo and talking about his mother had been a wrenching emotional experience. Their surge of passion, that moment of incredible closeness, had been the result of emotions suppressed throughout the years. It was the only possible explanation.

"We'd better—" he began.

"I think—" she started to say at the same time, then stopped because her voice sounded shaky and unlike her own.

A little man in a dark business suit, shoes squeaking with hurry, walked past them. He glanced curiously at them as Ken cleared his throat and tried again. "We'd better get moving if we want to get back to Shinjuku before dark."

They'd got all their signals mixed up, Randy realized. She'd reacted to Ken's pain by wanting to comfort him. She'd reached out to a child whose mother had been so cruelly taken from him. But Ken Sawa was no child.

Randy took a deep breath and swallowed hard, but the knot in her throat wouldn't go down, no matter how she tried. She was disgusted with herself. The kiss had been just an emotional response, a way of diffusing almost unbearable tension. It hadn't meant anything, and the sooner she forgot about it the better.

Randy had her eyes closed when the bullet train rolled into Shinjuku Station. They hadn't had much to say to each other as they waited at the station, and once they'd boarded, Ken had opened a newspaper. He'd offered Randy a section of the paper, but she had pleaded weariness.

Though she willed herself to fall asleep, she couldn't do so. Too many images danced behind her closed eyelids. Ken fencing with Tosa in the sunlit garden. Ken tucking that flower in her hair. Once again she felt disoriented by the remembered touch of his fingers, the warmth in his eyes. And then there was the feel of his lips—

"Shinjuku," Ken announced so abruptly that Randy's eyes snapped open. "I'm sorry if I startled you. I didn't think you were asleep."

"Actually I was going over my article in my mind. Today has been quite an experience."

In more ways than one— But he wasn't about to start rehashing his irrational behavior. Deliberately Ken folded his paper and thrust it under his arm. "Would you care for some dinner?" he asked politely.

"No, thanks. I'd best be getting back to the hotel."

"As you wish. I phoned the car from Kyoto, so it should be waiting for us."

"That's good."

Randy felt as though she and Ken were each hiding behind a protective force-field. Their conversation was stilted, almost mechanical, and they were careful to avoid touching each other as they traveled back to Asatsuki.

As they approached the hotel, the stifling politeness continued as Ken insisted on walking her to the door. "I hope the trip hasn't tired you too much," he said.

"No, not at all. Thank you so much for arranging the meeting with the *sensei*."

"Thank you for coming."

In another minute they'd be bowing to each other. Randy had turned and started to walk briskly toward the hotel when Ken said, "Randy."

She didn't want to stop walking, wasn't going to, but suddenly she found that she couldn't move. "Yes?" Randy said, and waited.

Ken felt suddenly at a loss. "About this afternoon," he began lamely.

"Nothing really *happened.*" Randy was proud that her voice sounded steady. She was in control. "Ken, neither of us are kids. It was just—"

"The heat of the moment?" he suggested.

"Maybe we both had too much tradition for one afternoon," she replied.

Her uncertain smile made something odd happen inside his chest. Almost desperately Ken reminded himself who Randy Muir was and about the article she was writing. He reminded himself why he'd taken her to Kyoto in the first place.

Just then the hotel doorman spotted them and swung open the door. Mechanically Randy stepped into the lobby. She was breathless, and her heart was drumming away like mad. All she wanted to do was to go up to her room and collapse on her bed.

"You're wrong about this afternoon." Ken had followed her through the door and was standing beside her in the lobby. "Something *did* happen."

She made the mistake of looking up at him, and the expression in his eyes caused the hairs on the back of her neck to stand up. It was as though she were surrounded by a smoldering brush fire just waiting to ignite. She held her breath as she heard him say, "I want you to know that your sympathy meant a great deal to me."

"Sympathy," the man called it, while her insides were quivering like unset jelly and her pulses had started with a Gene Krupa number. Her knees felt unsteady. Not trusting herself to speak, Randy nodded.

Would he go away now and leave her in peace? He would not. "We had a good day together," Ken was saying. "I didn't want to end it on a bad note."

"Ran-dee! Over here!"

Ken frowned at the interruption. The frown deepened to a scowl as he recognized the tiny young woman who had risen from one of the lobby chairs. With her was a thin man in a black suit.

"This is a surprise," Randy was exclaiming. "What are you and Shin-san doing in Asatsuki so late, Minny?"

"We phoned this afternoon, and the desk clerk told us you had gone to Kyoto with Sawa-san. So we came and waited for you to return."

Naturally, Ken thought cynically. The timing was perfect.

He'd have to hand it to Randy; she moved quickly. He'd given her short notice this morning, and yet she'd had time to arrange this "coincidental meeting" between him and her activist friends.

Unfortunately for her, he wasn't staying around for a confrontation. Ignoring Minako and Shin Naka, he nodded coldly to Randy. "Good night," he said.

His surface calm didn't fool her for a second—he was angry. Randy stiffened as she realized that Ken thought she'd set up this meeting. Before she could tell him that she'd never have been party to anything so sneaky, he was striding to the door.

With an exclamation of dismay, Shin Naka loped after him. "Wait, Sawa-san," he called. "Please wait."

Several people who were sitting around the lobby looked up in surprise. The clerk behind the desk craned his neck to see what was going on. Ken, who had reached the door, turned and stared frostily down at the earnest young man.

"Yes?" he snapped.

Shin blanched at his tone and took a step backward, bumping into Minako, who said firmly, "We would like to speak to you, Sawa-san. It would take only a moment of your time. We have been wanting to meet with you—"

"I regret that I'm busy right now," Ken interrupted. "Phone Yamazaki and set the meeting up for later this week."

Once more Ken started toward the door, but Minako stepped in front of him. "How long do you intend to put us off?" she challenged. "Why can't we have that meeting right now?"

Everyone in the lobby was staring at them. Ken knew that to refuse to listen to these nuisances would appear rude and cause him—and Sawa Industries—to lose face. Inwardly seething, he growled, "I'll give you exactly five minutes."

Unhappily Randy watched Ken stride over to a cluster of chairs and sit down. Would he believe her if she told him she hadn't been responsible for Minny and Shin being there? She caught his eye and stifled a sigh. Not likely.

Meanwhile, Shin had launched into an impassioned speech about Yoshitsune.

"Yoshitsune Minamoto is important to us modern Japanese," he cried. "He was loyal to his family. He was a poet and a gallant warrior. To destroy Yoshitsune's Rock would be to destroy the best of what Japan stands for."

Shin's voice was husky with emotion as he continued to talk about poetry, art and self-sacrifice. The stuffy young man really believed what he was saying. Ken, who had little use for the rock or the bogus legends that surrounded it, still felt a grudging admiration for Naka's sincerity.

When Shin finally wound down, Ken spoke in a quieter tone. "I understand what you're saying. All right, here's a compromise. If possible, I'll have Yoshitsune's Rock moved." Then, as Shin opened his mouth to speak, Ken added, "I'll have a geologist look into the matter and see if that's feasible."

Shin looked relieved, but Minako challenged, "Then you still intend to destroy Yui Hill?"

Ken's face hardened. "There's no way around that."

"Doesn't it bother you that you are killing something?" Minako shouted. "Killing *Ephemerum hygromatica* is as bad as slaughtering elephants. Perhaps worse, because elephants are big and beautiful and people will fight for their right to live. Not many people care whether or not a moss is destroyed."

"*I* care," Randy said.

Her low voice seemed to throb in the silence that had followed Minako's speech. Ken saw that she was sitting very still, her hands clasped in her lap. Her expression was deeply troubled.

"Isn't there *some* way that Yui Hill can be spared?" she asked Ken.

Oh, Randy, if only you knew.

Abruptly Ken got to his feet. "Major changes in the plans would affect too many people," Ken said. "However, I'll talk to my architects. *If* it is possible to spare some part of the hill—*and* your moss—I'll consider a minor alteration in the existing plans."

"That's all we ask," Minako breathed.

Nobody moved or spoke for a full minute after Ken left the hotel lobby. Then Minako clasped her hands to her chest. "It's more than I hoped for. Shin-san, you were so eloquent. You were magnificent!"

The thin young man was horribly embarrassed. "It was nothing," he stammered. "You were the brave one. I think that Lady Shizuka must have been like you."

Minako's narrow cheeks flamed with color. She ducked her head and produced a totally uncharacteristic giggle. "What nonsense you speak, Shin-san. It is you who must be admired."

Feeling like the proverbial third wheel, Randy said her good-nights and left them. As she climbed the stairs to her room, she tried to put things into perspective. Be real, she told herself sternly.

The problem was that reality meant different things to different people. Minny had her moss. Shin had his hero, Yoshitsune. Ken's reality was Sawa Town. "And for me it's *Issues Today* and my article," she reminded herself, "so get cracking, lady."

Late into the night she worked on her article, getting down her impressions of Umezono-*sensei* and his family. But though this article had richness and variety, it didn't *feel* right.

Time to backtrack, Randy told herself. Next day she set out again to talk to the people of Asatsuki.

This time she went without Minako to interpret for her. Though she couldn't understand all of what was said, Randy found that she preferred this one-on-one interaction. By the end of the week she had learned the in-depth thoughts of many people.

Shopkeepers and teachers, the town's one dentist, housewives and white-collar workers, laborers and even children knew who Kenjiro Sawa was. Over and over Randy heard variations of the same story. The Sawas had built a new hospital at Asatsuki. The old hospital was all right, but there hadn't been any modern facilities, and if you got really sick, you had to go to Ohashi to get treatment. The younger Sawa-san was also concerned about education. He'd donated several computers to the Asatsuki middle school. And when the primary school had its athletic event, he'd been right there cheering the youngsters on.

Randy's last interview was with Dai-suké, the proprietor of the noodle shop where she and Ken had once lunched. Since the noonday rush was over and the evening crowd had not yet arrived, Dai-suké was ready to gossip.

"Oh, I know the younger Sawa-san quite well," he boasted. "He's been coming to my shop ever since they started construction of Sawa Town. A fine man.

Doesn't turn up his nose even though he's rich and powerful."

"What is the elder Sawa-san like?" Randy wondered.

Dai-suké pursed his lips. "He is a very rich and important man, that's all I know. I only saw him once, when they had the ground-breaking ceremony for Sawa Town last year. I tell you, Randy-san, he didn't look well, even then. He was small and pale and thin, not like his son at all. Now, Kenjiro-san is a man to look up to."

"You mean, because of the hospital and the school and so on?"

"Well, sure, there's that. But beyond that, Kenjiro-san is a good man." Dai-suké plucked a toothpick from a handy jar and stuck it meditatively between his teeth. "I'll tell you a story not many people know," he confided. "My neighbor, Hanakawa, used to own the flower stall by the cooperative market. This winter he became ill—cancer, poor fellow—and Kenjiro Sawa-san found out about it. Would you believe he sent Hanakawa to a specialist in Tokyo and paid the bill?"

Apparently Ken had visited the ailing flower-seller several times, and before Hanakawa died had promised to give the man's oldest son a job at Sawa Industries. "So poor old Hanakawa died in peace," Dai-suké wound up. "With a good job like that, the boy could support the entire family."

It wasn't the first time Randy had heard about Ken's generosity. Her tape recorder was filled with instances where he had concerned himself with the people of Asatsuki. These incidents had all been private, without fanfare, so it wasn't publicity that Ken was looking for. But, Randy reminded herself, this didn't mean that Ken Sawa was a candidate for sainthood.

Dai-suké was still talking. "Sawa-san's done a lot for my business, too. When it was learned that he came here often, my customers trebled. And—*arré*, Sawa-san—you're either late for lunch or early for dinner."

Looking over her shoulder, Randy saw that Ken had entered the little shop. "Are you working?" he asked.

There was a definite edge to his voice, and the look he gave her tape recorder wasn't friendly. "I'm through here," Randy said as she returned her tape recorder to her shoulder bag and snapped shut her pen and notebook. "I won't interrupt your dinner."

But Ken hadn't come to Dai-suké's to eat. Earlier, en route to the office and a meeting with Yamazaki and the architects, he'd seen Randy go into the noodle shop. He'd found he couldn't concentrate on his work, had cut the meeting short and had walked over to Dai-suké's.

He had no clue as to why he was acting this way. Though it hadn't taken long for him to realize that Randy hadn't set him up the other night, he had decided it would be wise to avoid her company. Yet here he was, watching her stuffing her paraphernalia into her shoulder bag and feeling confused and irritated. Dammit, it wasn't as if he'd actually been *missing* the woman.

Why was he looking at her like that? Randy wondered. Her usually capable fingers had turned to butternut squash, and several tapes fell out of her bag, bounced on the counter and thence to the floor. She and Ken bent to retrieve the tapes at the same time.

There was a sharp crack as their heads collided. Randy yelped and Ken gasped, "My God, you have a hard head."

Randy massaged her aching skull. "Likewise."

They both began to laugh at the same time, and Dai-suké said solicitously, "Do you want some ice to put on your head, Sawa-san? That was a bad knock you got there. You might pass out or something."

Ken shook his head, dropped the rescued tapes back into Randy's bag and slid an arm through hers. "No, thanks. We'll totter out of here while we can walk."

"I can walk just fine," Randy said, but it was a lie. The familiar feel of Ken's arm through hers, the remembered press of his strong, lean body against her side, did things to her knees. She wanted to pull free of him, but he held her too firmly, and she didn't want to get into a tussle with him.

"Thank you for the interview, Dai-suké-san," she called.

The noodle shop proprietor grinned and replied in English, "You're welcome."

"I thought you'd finished with your interviews," Ken commented as they walked out into the late-afternoon sunshine.

His voice sounded pleasant and warm again. The constraints that had been with them since that scene in the alley had disappeared. Randy felt absurdly happy as she shook her head.

"The article hasn't come together yet."

She sounded breathless. They were standing so close that when she moved, he could draw in her subtle fragrance. She looked like a spring flower in her cream-colored jacket and matching slacks, with the slender gold-and-jade necklace at her throat.

He *had* missed her. He'd missed her very much. By all laws of reason and logic, Ken knew that he shouldn't have done so. They were on opposite sides of the controversy surrounding Sawa Town, which was the single most important thing in his life just now. For perhaps the hundredth time, Ken told himself that this was no time to even think of romancing this tough-minded, stubborn woman writer.

"Well," she was saying, "we seem to be in one piece. No concussion, no double vision, no bones broken. Our heads are harder than we thought."

Hardheaded logic was definitely what was needed here. Ken opened his mouth to wish Randy a polite goodbye and instead heard himself asking, "Are you going to view the cherry blossoms this weekend?"

"The—? No, I hadn't planned to."

"You should. They'll be in full bloom, and every Japanese worth his or her salt will be out viewing the flowers. *Hana-mi* is a national obsession." Ken paused. "It'd be criminal to be in Japan and not go on a cherry blossom pilgrimage."

She'd be returning to the States in a few weeks, and she had work to do. Besides, she'd admired the cherry trees in Washington, D.C. If you saw one cherry blossom, you'd seen them all.

"I'll pick you up at about ten o'clock Saturday," Ken was saying. "Is that all right?"

Randy made the mistake of meeting his amber gaze. She found herself hesitate, wavered, and was lost.

Aw, what the heck, she thought. Who was she to argue with a national obsession?

Chapter Seven

Ken had been right about one thing, Randy thought. Every living soul in Japan seemed to be thinking of cherry blossoms.

Breakfast this morning had featured something called a "cherry blossom set." She had ordered it out of curiosity and found it to be two slices of thick toast, a fat omelet set with a Japanese flag and fruit compote decorated with cherry blossoms. Then, when she'd come out to the hotel lobby, she found about fifty people wearing comfortable shoes, carrying cameras and video cameras and looking intent and expectant as they awaited a tour bus.

When Ken came to fetch her, driving a compact, late-model car instead of the office sedan, Randy noted that a group of children and their mothers were walking along the sidewalk. Some of the women and most of the little girls were dressed in kimonos.

"Can you wait a second?" she cried. "I'm going to ask them if I can take their photos."

Ken admired the lithe grace with which Randy sprinted across the street. Following his suggestions, she'd worn sneakers and jeans. Her amber shirt and fisherman's-knit sweater suited her, and her well-worn jeans hugged her long legs and the curve of her hips. Memory of stroking those well-rounded curves caused Ken's emotional thermostat to shoot into the danger zone.

He knew now that he was glad he'd offered to take her flower viewing even though he couldn't rationalize this move. The importance of keeping Randy from writing an uncomplimentary article hadn't justified the way his pulse quickened whenever he thought of her.

Ken's heartbeat quickened now as Randy returned to the car. "Did you run out of film?" Ken asked.

"Not a chance. I got all the photos I wanted *and* their consent to let me publish their photos in *Issues Today*. They're going to climb up Yui Hill. Apparently there's a grove of cherry blossoms near Yoshitsune's Rock."

She glanced at him to see his reaction to this, but all he said was, "Those trees are nothing to write home about. The Yoyama Gardens, on the other hand, are worth a drive."

"I've never heard of the Yoyama Gardens. Are they in the guidebook?"

"No, so we won't be crushed by thousands of people. You don't know how relentless the Japanese can be in their pursuit of beauty."

She settled comfortably into the seat. "Tell me more about the relentless Japanese."

"I'd rather talk about beauty. You look lovely today, Randy."

He wasn't just saying the words; he meant them, and the way he looked at her caused a warm shiver to slide through her bones. She took refuge in being flip. "I bet you say that to all the girls you take cherry blossom viewing."

Dark eyebrows slanted upward. "Are you kidding? I wouldn't dare say that to a Japanese woman. She'd dissolve with embarrassment, and I'd have to spend the day apologizing."

Randy realized that she'd missed Ken's smile, his humor. Darn it, she'd missed *him*.

She'd given up trying to figure out why. It was a given that he was a handsome male animal with more sex appeal than should have been legal, but that wasn't the reason she'd thought of him so often. He could make her laugh, but that wasn't it, either. He could be and was inflexible on certain matters. He could be devious. He was good and bad, sunlight and shadow, and she was drawn to him as she'd never been drawn to any man.

Ken was saying, "How is your article coming?"

"Not too well," Randy admitted. "I think it's because I'm too close to what I'm writing. When I get back to New York, I'll get my perspective back."

She would be going home in ten days—back to New York and her life there. Soon Asatsuki would be only a memory. She glanced at Ken's hard profile, and a thought flitted tentatively across her mind. Sternly she brushed it back. As she'd said, it was high time she got back her perspective.

"There's something I need to tell you," Ken said.

His serious tone broke through her thoughts, and she looked at him anxiously. "The geologists we consulted feel that Yoshitsune's Rock is too deeply embedded in the hill," he told her. "It can't be moved."

Poor Shin, Randy thought. Aloud she asked, "Is there some way to save a part of the hill?"

"Our architects are doing their best, but as I said before, I can't promise miracles." Abruptly Ken changed the subject. "Do you like jazz, Randy? There's a group I'd like your opinion on."

He had brought along a tape of a Japanese group, and they played some of the best jazz she'd ever heard. Ken knew the artists personally, and they were deep into a discussion about jazz when they left the main thoroughfare. The secondary highway onto which they turned was pitted and graveled, and Ken said, "Better hang on. It's going to be bumpy for a while."

This was an understatement. The car rattled and banged over what had to be the worst road that Randy had ever endured. "I'll never complain about potholes in New York again," she vowed through chattering teeth.

She gasped as a particularly horrendous bump sent her straining forward against her seat belt. Ken threw out his arm instinctively to protect her, saying, "Sorry—couldn't dodge that one."

The supporting line of his arm rested under her breasts for a second, and even when it was withdrawn, Randy found it hard to catch her breath.

"Are you all right?" he was asking.

"Sure, fine," she lied. "How long do we have to stay on this road?"

"We're almost there."

As he spoke, Ken pulled onto a narrow, paved path. "This looks like a private way," Randy noted doubtfully. "Are we trespassing?"

"Yoyama Gardens is owned by my family."

"You didn't tell me that!"

"You didn't ask." Ken halted his car in a clearing lined with Japanese maple and pine trees. Beyond the clearing rose a wooden fence so tall that only the tips of bamboo could be seen above it.

He got out of the car and came around to open her door. "Ready?" he asked.

He was holding out a hand to help her. Not to take it would have been churlish, but taking it was a disaster. The strong-gentle clasp she remembered sent slow-moving tendrils of warmth dancing through Randy's veins.

This couldn't go on. Under the pretext of taking out her camera, she rescued her hand. "Bring on the cherry blossoms," she quipped.

But as she followed Ken to the huge wooden door, Randy wasn't thinking of cherry blossoms. Her thoughts were on, of all things, the Sumire hotel. Her thoughts were— Randy stopped herself right there. She definitely didn't want to examine her thoughts or what they were doing to her.

"Want me to carry something?" Ken offered. "You look flushed."

But she was looking delicious. Ken found himself wanting to start with sampling her delectable mouth. Then he'd work downward to the creamy V of her neck, the swell of her breasts that a few moments ago had been pressed against his arm—

With more force than necessary, he pounded on the door. "Anyone in there?" he shouted.

"All right, all *right*—you don't have to break the door down," a querulous voice exclaimed. "I'm coming, aren't I?"

There were mumbles, creaks and jolts, and then the heavy door was flung open by an old man dressed in work clothes. He had on black gaiters and rubber boots, and a straw hat had been jammed over sparse gray hair. Beetling gray brows were knotted into a frown over faded but belligerent eyes.

"Why are you making all this noise?" he snapped. "This is private property."

Ken sighed. "Taka, how often do I have to tell you that you need eyeglasses?"

The old man blinked rapidly. "Kenjiro-sama?" he exclaimed. "But, young master, you should have telephoned me to say you were coming. Nothing is ready for you—"

Ken put both hands on Taka's shoulders and gave him an affectionate shake. "The last time I phoned you, you ran around like a madman making preparations. You got lumbago. You were in bed for a week, your married daughter had to come and stay with you and you were so miserable that you phoned me every day to complain that your life wasn't worth living.''

"Even so, you should have called," the old man wailed. "Bringing a lady guest to a place where there is nothing for refreshment—not even rice cakes—it's too bad of you, young master. I have lost face."

Ken and Randy spent five minutes convincing the old man that he had all the face in the world, that all they wanted to do was view the gardens. Even then, Taka wasn't mollified.

"I will take my bicycle and get some cakes from the cake shop," he announced. "No, young master, my mind is made up. What would your father think if he heard that I hadn't even offered you a cup of tea?" Taka paused to add anxiously, "How *is* the honored master? When last I heard, he was very ill with some horrible virus."

"He's better."

"But what was the matter with him?" the old man prodded. "Don't these foolish modern doctors know anything? When they aren't sure what ails a person, they say it's a virus. Ah, young master, you can say what you like, but acupuncture and cupping are good enough for me any day."

He was winding himself up to give a lecture. With some alarm Ken nudged Randy. "The cherry blossoms are that way," he said.

"And a fine sight they are, too," Taka interrupted. "I wish Junjiro-sama could see them." He added seriously, "When I heard Junjiro-sama was ill, I went to the Buddhist temple and paid the priests to chant prayers. Then I went to the Shinto shrine and invoked the ancestors' help, just in case they were listening. You never can tell with the honored ancestors.''

As he shuffled off toward a little house some distance from the gate, Randy exclaimed, ''Is he truly going to ride a bicycle? Ken, he'll never make it.''

''Go argue with the old buzzard,'' Ken growled. ''Even my father never won an argument with Taka.''

''Perhaps if you offer to drive to the cake shop...'' But Randy's words trailed off into silence as they walked through the line of pine trees. Before her lay a garden of incredible beauty.

It had been crafted like a glen between two miniature green hills, and from one of these hills tumbled a waterfall that emptied into a pool edged with calla lilies, iris and Japanese pampas. Around the pool the whitest sand had been raked smooth, and a pathway had been built around it. The subtle sounds of water falling created a perfect backdrop for the most exquisite cherry trees that Randy had ever seen.

''My great-uncle planted sixteen varieties of cherry blossoms,'' Ken explained. ''None of them bear fruit. Their only purpose in life is to be beautiful.''

Each tree was mounted with white and pale pink blossoms, and even to Randy's inexpert eye, each tree had been pruned and trained to be a work of art. Speech seemed inadequate, so she said nothing and instead kept looking around and discovering new delights. There was a stately stone lantern surrounded with bonsai pines, and an exquisitely shaped statue of the goddess Kwannon, goddess of mercy. At the goddess's feet was a handsome bronze sundial.

Randy walked over to admire it, and Ken followed her. "The sundial was Nora's idea. She loved this garden so much she'd lose all track of time."

Randy smiled. "Mom does that, too."

Oddly enough, she felt at home. Though the Yoyama Gardens were a hundred times more grand than her mother's, they held the same sense of peace and welcome.

Impulsively she exclaimed, "I wish I'd known your mother, Ken."

She would have loved you. He didn't speak the thought aloud, but Ken was conscious of the truth of it as he watched Randy wandering absorbedly around the garden. Hands clasped behind her back, she strolled under the trees where pale petals drifted down, forming a perpetually moving, changing curtain. "It's like looking up into pink clouds," Randy exclaimed.

"What's that?"

His voice had come from some distance away. Randy blinked, looked around and didn't see Ken anywhere. "Where are you?" she called.

"Over here—by the gazebo. Just follow the path around the pool."

She did as he said, and in a few moments the path of cherry trees opened to disclose a gazebo shaped like a miniature Japanese palace. It had obviously been built so that people could sit down and admire the flowers, for it had a roof but no walls, and thick straw mats had been spread on the wooden floor.

Randy looked around for Ken and was surprised to see him kneeling in a patch of green some distance from the gazebo. At first she thought he was performing some sort of religious ritual, but a closer look showed her that he was in a patch of weeds and wrestling with a large specimen.

Some distance from Ken was a wheelbarrow half-filled with uprooted weeds. "Taka must have been working here when we came," he commented. "This one's a stubborn beast."

"*Shikari-shite,* as everybody says around here. 'Hang in there.'" Randy walked over to the weed-patch and tugged at a weed. It didn't budge. "You're right," she said, "these guys won't give up without a fight. Ah—there's a hoe."

She removed her sweater and tossed it onto the gazebo floor before picking up the hoe that was lying near the wheelbarrow. "What do you think you're doing?" Ken protested. "I didn't bring you here to weed the garden."

"You forget my bucolic childhood. I learned to mash weeds before I could walk." Randy hefted her hoe. "Let me show you how it's done."

Ken's objections turned to amazement as he watched the weed go down before Randy's bold stroke. "Here, give me that," he exclaimed.

"Not on your life, mister. This is my hoe. If you want one, you find one." Randy uprooted another weed. "Hey, this is fun."

"You have weird ideas about fun," Ken grumbled. He found a shovel lying half-hidden in the weeds and went to work, saying, "Taka used to tell me that he was at war with the weeds. Now I know why."

"He seems like quite a character."

"He's a pain in the neck." Ken scowled as he tossed a large weed onto the wheelbarrow. "He's nearly blind, but he distrusts opticians and hates glasses. And he insists on taking care of the gardens himself without so much as an assistant. Sometimes I want to wring his neck, but he's been with the family since before I was born."

Randy said thoughtfully, "Maybe there's another way to skin the cat. I remember—" She saw that Ken was shaking his head. "What? What did I say?"

"Something tells me I'm about to hear another saga about the Muir clan."

"Can I help it if I have a large and colorful family? Listen up. My cousin Harris was getting too old to run his grocery store out in St. Louis, but he wouldn't hear of taking on 'help.' The day he grew too old to do his own work, he said, was the day he'd turn up his toes and die. It was a mess."

"I'm sure you did something clever."

"We did some checking around and found this strong young kid who really wanted to learn the grocery business firsthand. He went to Harris and begged, as a favor, to be allowed to watch a pro in action."

"And Harris bought it?"

"Sure, he bought it. Harris knew he needed help. He just needed to save face."

Ken frowned thoughtfully. "You may have something there." Then he added, "That's it for the weed pulling. If we pull them all, Taka will know we did it and die of shame."

Randy acknowledged the truth of this. "We've got the biggest ones, anyway. Is there someplace where we can wash up?"

There was an old-fashioned pump on the other side of the gazebo. Pulling weeds was hot work, and Randy was glad to roll up her shirtsleeves and wash her face and arms. "Can I drink the water?" she asked.

For answer, he cupped his clean hands, filled them with water and offered them to her. "You'll never taste anything better."

They'd been laughing and talking to each other so easily that she didn't think. But when her lips touched the mesh of his fingers, everything changed and she was aware of the warmth of his hands contrasting with the cool water. She felt his strength, and beyond that, a tenderness and sensitivity that took her breath away. When she could fill her lungs again, she inhaled not the faint fragrance of cherry blossoms but his virile, clean man-scent.

Her last gulp of water went down wrong, and she began to cough. He caught her around the waist, patting her back. "Are you okay?"

"Okay," she gasped, but that was a lie. The arm around her was doing crazy things to her body, and her mind was riding a roller coaster of memories and half-formed fantasies.

Ken was asking solicitously, "Do you want to sit down for a while?" He guided her toward the gazebo, adding, "After all, we drove all the way up here to admire the cherry blossoms."

Taking off his shoes, he stepped up onto the wooden floor, and after a moment's hesitation, Randy followed. Taking off her shoes, she stepped up onto the wooden floor. Old Taka had obviously been at work, for the floors had been polished, and the straw mats were clean.

Randy drew a deep breath and forced herself to stop coughing. She started to wipe her eyes with the back of her hand, but Ken drew out his handkerchief and did that for her. "Better?"

"Lots better." She attempted a bright smile and took a step away from him as though to look about her. "It *is* beautiful here."

"Then sit down and admire. My great-uncle used to invite his friends to come and sip sake and compose poems to the cherry blossom."

Ken sat down cross-legged on a mat and smiled invitingly up at her. Warily Randy sank down some distance from him. She wasn't going to look at him, she told herself. If she didn't look at him, she couldn't get into trouble.

"Did you write poems, too?" she asked.

"No. The flowers are poems in themselves."

His deep voice was a magnet, drawing her eyes. She wasn't going to look at him— But she did. The expression she saw in those golden depths made her catch her breath.

Ken heard that little intake of sound, and the world went so still that he could almost hear the fall of petals. Even the wind seemed to be holding its breath. The small space that divided him from Randy was electric, waiting.

He had to say something or do something to break the almost unbearable tension. "Randy," Ken began.

"What?" she whispered.

Whatever he'd meant to say, he didn't say it. Instead, he gathered her into his arms.

She fit into his arms as though she'd been made for that purpose. Her gently rounded curves rested lightly against his hardness. The lips that caressed his were as sweet as he remembered, and before he lost himself in their kiss, Ken realized that all week long he'd been living a lie. He'd been working and talking and going through the movements of living while all he'd wanted to do was to kiss Randy again.

She'd missed him. Randy knew the truth of that as their kiss deepened, as their mouths melded in single-minded passion. She'd wanted his arms around her, his lips pressed against hers. It was inescapable. Inevitable. She leaned into his arms and wrapped her arms around his neck.

His hands were busy, tracing erotic patterns over her back, dipping down to her hips and over her ribs, then sliding up to her breasts.

It was as though she'd been stroked by lightning. As Randy felt Ken's fingers trace the curve of her breast, she could feel her entire body change. No longer was she made of flesh and blood and bone but of liquid heat. Randy wanted to melt into the hard body that held her.

Her nearness was doing things to Ken that he could barely control. Things he didn't want to control. He felt drunk with the taste of Randy's mouth, and couldn't get enough of the taste and feel of her.

With a swift movement he drew the shirt out of her slacks and slid his hand against her bare back. Randy gasped at the contact of his cool hand against her fevered skin. Pleasure that was almost pain coursed through her, and she moaned a word against his lips.

"Ken, please—"

Please stop? Go on? She had no idea what she meant, what she wanted. It was as though she were caught in currents too strong for her. His lips were doing that, and the intoxicating brush of his fingers. His tongue explored the inside of her mouth, touching, tantalizing. At the same time, his hand moved from her back to her ribs, upward until it encircled the proud swell of her breast.

Even through the protective barrier of cloth, his touch burned. A slow, liquid heat slid through Randy's skin and into her blood. It invaded her veins and the bones she no longer seemed to have. Hardly realizing what she did, she slid her hand between the folds of his shirt until her fingers stroked the warm hardness of his chest.

It was like feeling steel layered with silk. But not silk exactly. Randy's questing fingers felt the fuzz of his chest hair, the cool, taut peaks of his male nipples. The feel of them as they hardened under her caressing fingers mirrored her own want.

Her hands on him were like butterflies. They tormented and pleasured him and set him on fire. Ken took his mouth away from Randy's to kiss the creamy V at the throat of her shirt. Her skin tasted like flowers.

She shuddered as his tongue tasted the cleft between her breasts. She murmured his name, and for a second he shifted away, but it was only to pull off his own shirt before he drew her close again. Now she felt his bare chest against her midriff. Smooth, cool skin and hair and cotton— The mixture of textures was incredibly erotic as he lowered her to the floor.

The mats were cool against her back, but his weight was warm. Her legs were captured between his. Randy was lost in a sensation of being caught in a riptide that was too strong for her to resist. It was sweeping her away, out to sea, and she couldn't hold back any longer. And did she even want to try and hold back?

Yes. No. She wasn't sure.

What she was sure about was that she wanted Ken. She wanted to be with him in every way that mattered. What harm would it do if she gave in to the riptide? Nobody would be hurt if she and Ken made love here in this enchanted garden.

But after they made love, then what? The question forced itself against Randy's passion-hazed mind. After they made love, could she ride the riptide back to safety?

The answer wasn't reassuring. Beyond today, beyond this magical moment in this garden of flowers, there could be nothing else. After Ken and she made love, they would kiss and part.

Without realizing what was in her mind, Ken noted the change in Randy's body language. The willing, lithe body in his arms had tensed, and all of a sudden she was a hundred miles away. "What is it?" he whispered.

He took one arm from around her, cupped her chin in his hand and looked down into her eyes. "What, Randy?" he asked.

The gentleness in his voice was her undoing. It penetrated to the deepest, most hidden part of her being. She was in danger, but the danger came from herself and not from him. Once she let herself go, the riptide and the storm were waiting for her.

Ken knew that Randy's body was pulsing with shared desire. He looked down at her, saw that her mouth was swollen with his kisses. Her breathing was ragged. She really wanted to stay here, with him, but at the same time, she was afraid.

His own body, almost painful with passion, made his voice husky as he said, "You know I'd never do anything to hurt you. Randy, I'm crazy about you."

And she was crazy about him. It sounded like some song from the fifties' hit parade, Randy thought disjointedly. But being crazy about someone, wanting someone, was all right only if those two people could kiss and enjoy each other and then walk away without scars or wounds.

Ken bent to kiss her lips lightly. He kissed the tip of her nose, her eyelids. "You know I want you. You want me— Or am I wrong?"

"No, you're not," she replied honestly. "But Ken, I'm not sure this will work. I'm not one for casual affairs."

His smile was tender, a little wry. "There's nothing casual about what we feel for each other."

"I'm leaving in ten days."

"So? The world's a small place." He caught her hands and kissed the palms. "New York's not that far away, love. Why deny ourselves pleasure and happiness? We're both adults."

You're an adult, Randy. Surely you can see it my way? Nate's words, used when he'd tried to convince her that they both wanted a childless marriage, came out of nowhere and edged themselves into her passion-hazed mind.

She hadn't been taken in by Nate's devious ways, but she wasn't dealing with Nate now. Ken was more dangerous than Nate. He was like no one she'd ever known before, and if she once let him make love to her, she might never be able to forget him or be the same woman she'd been. Besides, Ken, too, wanted something from her, didn't he? Though she didn't doubt his desire for her, she also understood that his bringing her to these gardens had been part of his game plan to influence her article.

"Don't let a perfect day end like this," Ken was saying softly.

Randy made the mistake of looking into his golden eyes, and her reason wavered. All she really wanted was to go back into his arms.

But she held back, and Ken hesitated. Though he wanted to enfold her in his arms and kiss away her doubts, he'd realized that the shadows were back in Randy's eyes. When they made love, he didn't want those shadows between them.

Troubled, Ken let her go and watched Randy arrange her shirt back into her jeans. He saw that her usually steady hands were trembling, and was suddenly swept by a need, an urgency to connect with her again.

Words he'd wanted desperately to say before this but had never meant to say rose to his lips. "Randy, there's something I must tell you—"

There was a banging noise somewhere in the distance, and Taka's muffled voice shouted, "Hello, honored guests, where are you? I've finally come back from the cake shop."

Chapter Eight

Randy dragged the paper out of her typewriter, wadded it into a ball and tossed it into the already overflowing wastepaper basket.

Breakfast had been half a grapefruit and black coffee. Lunch had been delivered to her door by a waitress who whispered, *"Shikari-shite kudasai"* before tiptoeing out.

Now Randy whispered the words to herself, "Hang in there." It was past dinnertime, but she didn't feel hungry. There was an ache someplace in the middle of her spine, her neck hurt and her head had been throbbing for the past hour.

Randy stretched her back, then spotted the evening paper that had been pushed underneath her door by the efficient chambermaid. She got up, picked it up and found herself staring at a photograph of Ken.

Randy sat down on the edge of her bed and frowned at the paper. Even in black and white, the man projected charisma.

Though she hadn't seen him since their trip to the gardens three days ago, Ken had haunted her thoughts. She couldn't see a tall man pass by or hear a deep voice without a suspicious leap of pulse. And if that weren't bad enough, the "shogun's" son even pursued her into her dreams.

She might as well admit the worst, Randy thought gloomily. Ken was the reason why her article was driving her up the wall. When she'd tried to write about the Umezonos, she'd remembered Ken tucking the flower into her hair. She'd attempted to contrast the so-called love hotel with the beautiful old Japanese inn—and found herself fantasizing about lying on flower-strewn sheets with Ken. Whenever she started to write, he would surface in her thoughts. Drat the man. If she didn't know any better, she'd say she was in love with him.

Impatient with such thoughts, she refocused on the newspaper article. There was a smaller figure standing beside Ken, and Randy blinked when she realized that this was Junjiro Sawa.

The president and founder of Sawa Industries had put on weight. In fact, his face looked bloated. Junjiro was smiling for the benefit of the camera, but he looked strained.

The Sawas had been photographed in Ashiya while attending a private dinner given in honor of a South American president. It was, Randy read, the first time the "shogun of modern industry" had appeared publicly since he'd been felled by a virus last November. That was probably why he looked so ill.

Randy put the paper down, walked restlessly over to the window and looked at the dark street below. She felt vaguely claustrophobic and tense. What she needed was a brisk walk. All she had to do was to pull a sweater over her shirt and jeans, slip on her sneakers and go.

She glanced at herself in the bureau mirror and frowned at her image in the glass. She'd skinned her hair back in a ponytail so that it would be out of the way, and she wasn't wearing a bit of makeup. Well, so what? she reasoned. She wasn't about to meet anyone she knew at this time of night.

As she stopped at the desk to leave her key, the clerk said, "Honored guest, there is a phone message for you from Sawa-san. When he heard that you were working on your article, he commanded us not to disturb you."

The phone call had come in around five o'clock, and the message simply said, "There's something I need to discuss with you. Please phone me at your convenience."

Randy glanced at her watch and saw it was edging on to nine o'clock. "He gave his home number at the Happiness building," the helpful clerk pointed out. "If you wish to phone now—"

"No," Randy interrupted him. "No, thank you. I'll wait."

She hadn't liked the way her heart went into its Gene Krupa number when she'd learned who the caller had been. She refused to admit that she wanted to phone him immediately. Ken could wait until she'd taken her walk, she told herself. After all, she wouldn't be long.

Outside the hotel, the night was cool and spring-time fresh. The moon was nearly full, and Randy couldn't help picturing cherry blossoms under its silver glow. The cherry blossoms in the Yoyama Gardens, for instance— Hastily, Randy began to walk.

In the distance, silhouetted against the moonlight, she could see the rise of Yui Hill. Randy frowned at it. Ever since Shin and Minny had learned that the rock couldn't be moved, they'd talked about nothing else. Shin was inclined to believe that Ken was trying to save a portion of the hill, but Minny believed that the Sawas were stringing them along with empty promises. According to Minny, Ken was going to have the hill destroyed before the opposition could do anything about it. And in case she was right, Minny declared, the Historical Environmentalists were ready. They were going to hold a vigil that would knock the socks off the Sawas.

Randy stopped dead in her tracks as she realized that tonight's phone call could very well have been about Yui Hill. Regretting that she hadn't returned Ken's call at once, she started to walk back the way she'd come. Then an idea came to her.

As a journalist, she knew that though the phone was an indispensable tool, it was also often impersonal. Ken could more easily be evasive over the phone. If, as she feared, his news was bad, he might not answer her questions, might even cut her short. Supposing that instead of phoning Ken she went to see him?

Once again Randy's heart did its flip-flop thing, but she ignored it. Her visit would not be personal, after all. She was going to see Ken on a purely professional level and for the sake of her friends.

Naked, Ken knelt beside the sunken tub of fragrant cedarwood and tested the water.

It had been a miserable day. His head ached, his neck had a crick in it and there was a raw feeling in his gut that wouldn't go away. Though there were a thousand things he ought to be doing, right now he didn't want to think about any of them.

The water tested out to be almost scalding hot—the perfect temperature for a Japanese-style bath. He had already soaped and washed and showered in the traditional Japanese way, and now he meant to relax.

Liquid heat flowed about him, releasing the natural fragrance of the wooden tub and caressing his limbs. Ken could feel his muscles yield to the stroking of the water, but the knot in his stomach remained ugly and twisted.

He glanced at his wristwatch, which he'd propped on the lip of the tub. Beside the watch was a paper and a telephone. Nine o'clock, he thought, and Randy hadn't yet phoned.

He respected her dedication to her work. Any article she wrote would mean more than just an assignment because the people connected with the issue would become important to her. That was what made Randy such a good writer. It also made her dangerous.

Ken swore suddenly and violently, and his frustrated roar was amplified by the silence. Though the Happiness building housed more than three hundred of Sawa Industries's employees, his suite on the fifth floor seemed inordinately quiet tonight.

Not liking the silence, Ken picked up the phone that sat beside the bath and punched out a number. "Yama?" he said as a familiar voice answered on the second ring. "Don't forget to bring the file on Yui Hill to the office tomorrow."

"I'll do better than that, I'll bring them by immediately," the office manager exclaimed. When told that Ken was relaxing in his bath, he added, "I won't bother you, Sawa-san. The door is unlocked, isn't it? I'll just leave the file on your living-room table."

He'd thought that talking with Yama would ease his mood, but the reverse was true. Ken hung up the phone feeling even more depressed. Impatient with himself, he reached for the newspaper he'd put down next to his watch and found himself frowning down at a photograph of himself and his father.

The knot inside Ken hardened into raw pain. The old man had always been brown and sturdy and lean. He'd been an avid golfer. Now his skin had a yellowish tinge, and the steroids were making his face swell. No one who looked at Junjiro could doubt that he was very ill. No one, that is, except for Junjiro himself.

Junjiro thought that he was so sick because of a virus he couldn't shake. He believed that he'd caught that bug while he was recuperating from an operation to remove his gall bladder. He was unaware of the cancerous tumor—inoperable and virulent—that remained in his stomach.

He didn't know the truth because the family had decided not to tell him. Grieving himself, Ken had argued against this decision, saying that a man like his father had a right to honesty. The elders in the family—Junjiro's older brother, Tomohiko, his elder sister, Yasuko—had opposed this view. They felt that to tell Junjiro Sawa about his terminal cancer would cause him unnecessary pain.

"Let him enjoy his life while he can," Uncle Tomohiko had decreed. "We will say nothing to him. Perhaps the new, experimental treatment that the doctors are trying will help. In the meantime, Kenjiro, you are to make his last days happy by building Sawa Town. It is your father's dream to see it completed, so you must build it with all possible speed."

Before the assembled family, Ken had vowed that he would do all he could to fulfill his father's greatest dream. At the time he hadn't thought there'd be a problem, but of course Murphy's Law had prevailed.

When he'd returned to Asatsuki, the Greater Kanto Historical Society had come out of the woodwork with their idiotic legend, and the botanists from the university had followed. Ken could have gone ahead and destroyed Yui Hill in spite of their objections, but that would have given the Sawas bad publicity and caused Junjiro grief. So, the forms had to be obeyed. The botanists and the historians had to present their petitions, and though he had no intention of going along with them, Ken had to pretend to consider their demands. Then, just when things had calmed down, he had met Randy.

Randy. When he recalled the way he'd seen her last, emerald eyes and silky black hair, the curve of her breasts soft against the gold of her blouse, his internal temperature rivaled the heat of the bath. Ken moved restlessly, causing water to slosh onto the marble floor. Dammit, he didn't want to think of Randy. But when he tried to recapture his thread of thought, he found that those threads were inextricably wound around her. Randy had stirred up the botanists and the historical society again, and there'd been more delays. That was when he'd decided to try to keep her from writing an article that might cause Junjiro pain— or throw a shadow on his memory.

The plan had backfired. Last weekend, at the Yoyama Gardens, he'd come within an inch of telling her about his father's illness. After that, Ken had carefully avoided even speaking to Randy. That is, until tonight.

Ken frowned as he considered the news he had to give her, but his face cleared when there was a knock on the bathroom door. Good old Yama had come as promised and brought the file with him. Ken's spirits lifted as he thought of sharing sake and a game of Japanese chess with his old friend.

"Yama," Ken called, "come in here."

The door opened and Randy stood there. She looked as stunned as Ken felt.

His outer door hadn't been locked, and the stereo had been playing. When she'd heard Ken's muffled invitation from behind the solid-teak door, she'd thought she was walking into his study. Randy hadn't dreamed of finding the man in his bath.

There he was, sprawled out in the steamy water. His dark hair gleamed like wet silk, and his powerful torso was like rain-licked marble. A coal black line of chest hair slid down to a narrow waist, lean belly— Hastily Randy averted her eyes.

"I'm s-sorry," she stammered. "The night watch-man told me to come up. I had no idea—"

His first impulse had been to lunge for a towel. But he'd tossed that towel into a basket by the door, and any movement on his part would probably send Randy shrieking into the streets. Moving casually so as not to alarm her, Ken sat up in the tub.

"Will you get the door?" he asked. "The win-dow's open, and there's a draft." He winced as Randy, who was backing out as he spoke, collided with the door. "Just close it, don't break it."

How could he be so calm? If anyone had walked in on *her* while she was taking a bath— But then, this was Japan. Belatedly Randy recalled that in Japan public bathing was no big thing. There were family bathhouses where respectable people routinely went to take their nightly ablutions, and families bathed to-gether, for Pete's sake.

Trying to salvage some of her dignity, she said, "I'm sorry. I should have phoned first. I'll talk to you later—"

"Wait," he said.

For a moment when he'd seen Randy standing there in the open doorway, Ken had thought that his fe-vered imagination had conjured her up. Now he real-

ized that she was very real and about to take to her
heels at any moment. He also realized that he didn't
want her to go.

At least not until he'd told her his news. Aloud he
said, "How have you been?"

Relieved that he sounded so calm and matter-of-
fact, Randy said, "I got your message saying that you
wanted to speak to me. I thought that I'd come and see
you instead of phoning. Sorry—it was a bad move."

"Don't worry about it, it's all right." Ken had
stopped feeling tired, and his depression had disappeared. Also, Randy's presence had caused him to feel
strong and vibrant again. Maybe too much so. Ken
added hurriedly, "If you'll wait outside a second, I'll,
ah, slip into something more comfortable. Then we
can talk."

That was what she'd come for—to talk. "Fine,"
Randy said, and walked hastily out of the bathroom.

She felt hot all over and not just from steam, either.
To get herself in hand, she looked about her at Ken's
living room. It was furnished in the Western style and
had the understated elegance that characterized Ken
himself. Randy approved of the clean, modern lines of
the teak furniture, the unobtrusive entertainment
center and bar. Fine watercolors and Utamaro prints
ornamented the wall above the white leather couch.

Next to the couch was a coffee table. On the table,
beside a thick, official-looking file, was a photograph
in a silver frame. Randy picked it up and looked down
at a fair-haired woman and a much younger, slimmer
Junjiro. Ken's parents. The woman had Ken's eyes and
smile.

The bathroom door opened and Ken appeared. "How did you get here?" he asked.

Randy had been sure she was back in control until she turned to face him. He was dressed in a navy-and-white cotton kimono that was tied at his lean waist. It clung to his still-damp body. Under the flow of cloth she could easily visualize the muscular form she'd just seen.

"I took a cab," she managed. "As I said, I should have phoned you."

He sat down in a chair across from her and watched her brush back a strand of hair. Her uncharacteristic nervousness lent her a vulnerability that made him ache to put his arm around her. "I'm glad you're here," he began.

His eyes, golden in the dimly lit room, told her that he meant it. Randy felt an answering spurt of joy that she immediately quenched. Naturally he was glad she was there—he'd wanted to talk to her, hadn't he?

"What was your phone call about?" she asked.

"First tell me how you've been. I've missed you."

He hadn't meant to say that, but once the words had come blurting out of him, Ken realized that they were true. He'd missed Randy so much she'd been haunting his waking and sleeping moments. Unsure of how she would react to his impulsive statement, he hastily added, "Have you been working night and day?"

She nodded. "Like you, I'm on a tight time frame."

"Then you need to relax." He got up and padded barefoot to the bar. "Will you try some sake?"

A drink might make him relax and talk more—and her nerves could do with some calming, too. "Why not?" Randy agreed.

"It'll take a second to warm the sake," Ken said. "So. How is the article coming?"

"Not well," she admitted.

"Take it from me, sake is the best thing for writer's block." He came over to her carrying a tray on which were a vaselike flask crafted from black-and-gold lacquer, and two tiny lacquer cups. Ken set the tray down on the coffee table. Seating himself next to Randy, he poured sake into her cup. "To your good health," he said.

"Aren't you pouring for yourself?" she asked.

"It's polite to fill a guest's cup but not your own. A host has to sit with his tongue hanging out until his guest takes pity on him."

Randy picked up the little flask and found it pleasantly warm to the touch. As she leaned over to fill Ken's glass, her arm brushed his.

"Watch it—don't spill it," Ken warned. He lifted his cup and toasted her. "To you."

She tipped the thimbleful of liquid to her lips and felt it trace a fiery path down her throat. Instantly he filled her cup again. "Whoa," she protested. "I've heard that sake is potent stuff. *You* have some."

He held up his cup, and she filled it once more. "Your hands aren't steady," he accused. "You need to relax, Randy. You should try a hot bath."

Was there an invitation in his deep voice? Randy said firmly, "I'll have one when I get back to the hotel."

"By that time your muscles will have hardened into a cramp."

Before she realized what he was doing, he'd shifted on the couch and had his hands on her shoulders. Her involuntary protest turned into a yelp of pain. "Ow—what do you think you're doing?"

"Loosening your muscles," he replied. "Lighten up, woman. You're in good hands."

"I don't need to have my muscles loosened—" Randy began, but he interrupted.

"Yes, you do. There's a knotted muscle right there." Her reaction was a muted howl. "Hurts, doesn't it? Comes from stress, as I said."

Randy felt as though she were one throbbing, palpitating mass of nerves. As he ran his hands lightly down her shoulders, she shivered.

"Massage in Japan is an old art, Randy. It doesn't just knead muscles, but transmits energy from one person to another."

He let his hands rove in slow circles along her shoulders and back. There was no demand in his touch, no urgency. All Randy felt was warmth that radiated throughout her.

Her eyelids closed. The heat, or electricity, or energy that was flowing out of Ken's hands was working. Incredibly all her aches and tensions eased, and she could feel herself sink into relaxation. It was as though layers of weariness were being peeled away from her.

"Feel good?" he queried.

"Mmm."

"Of course, it'd be better if you didn't have your clothes on."

Her eyes snapped open, and he clicked his tongue. "Anybody tell you you have a dirty mind? All I meant is that energy transmits more easily from skin to skin. Take off your sweater, at least."

He was right, Randy thought. Without her bulky sweater, the warmth of his hands felt even better. Randy sighed as Ken's fingers left her shoulders and traveled up her bare neck. Lightly, so lightly that Randy could hardly feel the touch, they stroked upward to the backs of her ears, around them and over her earlobes.

The streams of contentment that had been flowing through her halted in midtrack. The warmth and well-being she'd been experiencing changed and regrouped into a sensuous tingling. When Ken ran his fingers over her throat, she felt the stroke of them deep in her bones.

Randy gulped, hard.

Pulsing rivers of heat were now flowing from Ken's fingers. They seeped into her skin and turned the cool blood in her veins to smoldering pools. His fingers were like fiery feathers, caressing, teasing.

"Just relax."

Ken wasn't sure whether he was talking to Randy or to himself, because he was definitely in trouble. The texture of Randy's skin and the subtle, flower scent of her were like an aphrodisiac. It was torture to keep touching her like this when all he wanted to do was gather her into his arms.

Some die-hard instinct in Randy's brain was shrieking that she should jump up and go right *now*. But it was too late. There was no way she could move as knowingly, sensuously, he massaged her arms, her wrists, her fingers, the sensitive palms of her hands—

"Ah, Randy," Ken whispered.

The longing in his voice touched her more deeply than could any physical caress. Obeying an instinct stronger than mere reason, Randy leaned back into Ken's arms.

This time their kiss was different. It was like a storm, an earthquake. It destroyed all known boundaries and marooned the two of them in some unknown universe where the only reality was their need of each other. As Ken continued to kiss her with aching passion, Randy felt her body flame into response.

He was caressing her as if he'd been starved of her touch. His hands limned her shoulders, her arms, and then slid over her ribs and upward to brush her breasts. As his shadow-touch grazed the clothed tips of her breasts, Randy felt as though her skin and bones had begun a meltdown. Yearning, so strong that it was almost painful, spasmed through her.

Her gasp of reaction all but snapped what was left of Ken's self-control. It seemed as though all his tensions, all his frustrations and tangled emotions, had coalesced into throbbing need.

Shifting his weight, he drew her around on the couch to face him and rained small kisses over her eyes, her temples, her chin and back to her mouth. Meanwhile, his hands were running down her back, under her shirt. Murmuring incoherently, he pressed

her against him, and Randy could feel the force of his
desire through his kimono.

Still kissing her, Ken began to work her shirt but-
tons free. The intoxicating softness of her slender
body sent need spasming through him, and his heat
fueled her own. Brushing aside the folds of Ken's kimono, Randy trailed her fingertips over Ken's powerful chest.

Her hands were like burning butterflies, Ken
thought groggily. Meanwhile, his own hands and lips
seemed to have a life of their own. The hollow of her
throat felt like silk and tasted of honey, and the valley
between her breasts was like flower-scented satin.

"Sweet," he murmured. "So sweet, love."

He tasted faintly of salt. Randy ran her tongue
lightly over Ken's neck and, lifting herself a little out
of his arms, began to run her lips over his shoulder.
Ripples of steely muscles cloaked in silk welcomed her
caresses, and when she tasted his male nipples, the
small peaks tautened under her tongue.

"Randy," he groaned. "Do you know what you're
doing to me?"

What *she* was doing to *him?* Randy felt as weak as
a day-old kitten. There wasn't a muscle or a sinew
anywhere in her body that wasn't under siege. She felt
almost dizzy with want.

"Randy, my sweet love, it'll be good for us. Let me
make love to you—" Ken's words were disjointed,
hardly made sense, but Randy understood everything
he was saying and more besides. She wanted him. She
needed Ken to make love to her. But it wasn't just

about hunger and passion, though heaven only knew there was enough of that, too.

Randy's hair had come loose and hung like a silky dark curtain around them both as she leaned forward to touch Ken's chest with her lips. It wasn't just an act of passion, either. Randy felt as though her heart was passing through her lips into Ken's.

Because if this wasn't love, she didn't know a name for what she was feeling. The emotions that were inside her went beyond mere passion, further than desire. She was in love with Ken, had been for a very long time.

He was falling in love with her. As Randy's lips touched the area over his heart, Ken realized the truth that he'd been trying to hide from himself. He began to draw her close to him, but instead of crushing her, he enfolded her carefully. He needed to make love to Randy, and yet at the same time all he wanted to do was to cherish and protect her. She was dear and precious, and he wanted her so much that he was coming apart.

Ken's voice was hushed as he asked, "Randy?"

"Yes."

With her lips forming the word against his cheek, he lowered her onto the couch. As he did so, Ken's elbow caught the file that had been on the table. It fell to the floor.

In falling, the file brushed Randy's cheek. Instinctively she turned to glance at it and glimpsed an eight-by-ten-inch photograph. She started to turn away and then realized that it was a photograph of Yui Hill— Yui Hill with a large, distorting red X penciled over it.

"Let it alone, love, it's not important," Ken whispered.

He was stroking her, caressing her, and the touch of his fingers was magic. Randy willed herself to give in to that sweet sorcery, to forget what she'd seen. But when she closed her eyes, the hill with its disfiguring X leapt back into her mind.

"Ken," she said, and when he wouldn't listen, pleaded, "Ken—please stop."

This time he heard her. Pulling back, he asked, "Did I hurt you?"

"No." Randy drew a deep breath and husked, "It's just that—that photograph on the floor—Ken, have you decided to destroy Yui Hill?"

Chapter Nine

In the heavy silence that followed, Ken damned Yama for leaving the file on the coffee table. He damned himself for not seeing it there and removing it. He wished he'd never heard of the godforsaken hill.

He also wished that Randy would stop staring at him like that. "*Are* you going to destroy it?" she was repeating.

Her voice was troubled, light years away from the one in which she had whispered her desire for him. Reluctantly Ken drew away from her and sat up on the couch. "Our architects feel that we have no choice," he began.

Randy felt cold, which wasn't surprising since her shirt was gaping open to the waist. She pulled the edges of her shirt together as she whispered, "I see."

The soft lighting of the room did nothing to gentle the power of his muscular shoulders and bare back. It hardened his frown. "I didn't make any promises, Randy. I said I'd do what I could."

So this was the news he'd meant to give her. Randy felt an ache in her throat as he continued, "I wanted to tell you personally, which is why I left a message at the hotel."

But when she'd walked in on his bath, he'd decided to tell her *after* he'd gotten what he wanted. The ugly thought brought with it waves of self-disgust. How easily she had gone along with his plans.

Ken was saying, "I was just trying to find the right time to tell you."

She just looked at him.

"I'm sorry about the hill, Randy," Ken continued, "but surely you realize that it has nothing to do with what we feel about each other. I care deeply about you."

His voice could still stir embers of passion, but now she knew better than to give way to his blandishments. Ken was only sorry because his ploy had failed and he hadn't gotten her into his bed. Randy wasn't sure with whom she was angrier—Ken for being the manipulative cad he was, or herself for falling for his line.

"I should have known better," she muttered. "Dammit, I *did* know better."

Her attitude was making it difficult for him to keep his cool. Ken shrugged himself back into his kimono, took a deep breath and tried to stay calm and reasonable. "Our architects felt that changing the blueprints to go around the hill would cause incalculable delay—"

''And you couldn't let a small thing like conscience hold up your schedule,'' she interrupted.

''Dammit,'' he gritted, ''will you give it a rest? It's just a hill. A lump of mud. We're talking about a moss nobody cares about and a rock involved in a bogus legend.''

This was the Ken Sawa she had first met. He'd infuriated her back then, but now her anger was tinged with pain. ''I understand,'' Randy said.

How could she understand unless she knew the truth? Ken had never felt so torn. He wanted badly to tell Randy why Sawa Town *had* to be built without delay. He wanted to wipe the hurt, betrayed look from her eyes. But if he did tell her about his father, and the news leaked out—

He couldn't take that chance.

And besides, didn't she know him by now? Did she think that he'd been trying to use her like the clod who had put those shadows in her eyes? Anger blazed up in Ken, momentarily blocking out the hurt, and as Randy got to her feet, he snapped, ''Shall I call you a taxi?''

''Don't trouble yourself,'' she retorted coldly. ''The night watchman can do it. But don't count Yui Hill out just yet. It's not over till it's over.''

Eyes like frozen chunks of amber locked with hers. ''Meaning?''

''Minny and Shin are realists. They knew you'd destroy Yui Hill, so they've planned a vigil.''

He replied impatiently, ''They can stand vigil until hell freezes over. Yui Hill is being flattened at the end of the week.''

She must have been crazy to think she could have cared for this man. Randy took refuge in anger. "Fine. In any case, I'll be there to record the event for *Issues Today*."

He rose from the couch and stood glaring down at her. "If you're planning another media event, forget it. That damned hill is on private property, and I'll arrest every one of the demonstrators for trespassing."

She jeered, "I should've expected strong-arm tactics from you."

Emerald eyes blazed into his. She looked like a tigress about to do battle. There was no trace of the woman he'd held in his arms a few moments ago, the woman whom he had dreamed about. The woman with whom he'd thought he was falling in love. Ken wanted to shake Randy and at the same time wanted to kiss her hard enough to wipe that sneer from her lips.

His head had begun to throb with pain. He rubbed the temples with his thumbs, but the ache only got worse. "If any of those fanatics get up on the hill," he warned, "they'll be dragged down. Some of them might elude the police and hide up there—"

"Good for them," she cried.

"Not so good if they get hurt. We're using dynamite to break down that hill." He paused to add grimly, "All right, I'll compromise. As long as there are no press and no TV cameras, I'll allow the vigil around the base of the hill."

"That's really good of you!"

She was a headstrong nuisance. She was also so beautiful it twisted his heart. But that facet of their relationship was dead and buried, Ken reminded himself. After tonight, Yui Hill would always be between them.

"Perhaps I'll see you at the vigil," she was saying. "Of course I mean to be there."

"Who am I to stop you?"

His tone was hard with what she took to be sarcasm, but when she met Ken's eyes, Randy was surprised. Instead of the rage she'd expected, there was something like sadness in that golden gaze.

That inexplicable expression took her aback, and all of a sudden she wasn't sure of herself. But then he said, "Tell your friends that they'd be wise to play the game my way. They may think they have right on their side, but I have the law. They can't hold their vigil if they're all in jail."

His voice was cold. Whatever emotion she might have imagined had been wiped from his eyes, which were as inflexible as steel. In that moment Randy actually hated him. Ken was manipulative, controlling, arrogant and insufferable. He was incapable of real emotions.

She was grateful to have finally seen him in his true colors, Randy told herself. Now she could put an end to what never should have begun.

When Randy returned to the hotel, she phoned her friend. "I know it's late," she apologized, "but I have bad news."

"It must be about Yui Hill," Minako replied hoarsely. "I have the sore throat and a fever and cannot talk. Please to tell your news to Shin-san, Ran-dee. He has come to bring me his mother's medicine for the bad cold."

Shin, when he got on the phone, took the news calmly. "We were afraid that this would happen, so we've made all the arrangements for the vigil. The Historical Environmentalists will be ready."

Randy promised that she, too, would be present at the vigil. "But will Minny be all right?" she wondered.

"My mother makes a broth by pouring boiling water over grated burdock root and soybean paste," Shin assured her. "It has never failed."

But when the day of the vigil rolled around, Minny looked terrible. She still had a fever, and there were dark lines under her eyes. She could hardly talk.

"You should be in bed," Randy exclaimed. Minako shook her head fiercely, winced, then closed her eyes. "Go home," Randy urged. "Shin can run things without you."

Minny rasped. "Shin-san and I have a plan."

She tried to explain what this plan was, but talking hurt too much. Randy went to ask Shin and found him organizing the many dozens of people who had arrived for the vigil. Dressed in white, the demonstrators carried candles set in hurricane lamps.

"The candles will be lit when the sun goes down," Shin explained. "Also, at sunset Minako-san and I will take turns going up the hill and standing vigil beside Yoshitsune's Rock.''

"What if the Sawas have you arrested?"

"Then we will go to jail. People must be ready to suffer for what is important." Shin then added that no one else was going to climb the hill. "We do not want our friends to be arrested, but Minako-san and I are leaders of the group and must take risks. We will keep vigil by the stone all night."

Randy spent the afternoon photographing sympathizers and curiosity seekers, as well as those who had come to take part in the vigil. She interviewed many people and got their reactions on tape. No one bothered her, but she noted that Sawa Industries's security detail, as well as local police, had kept away all other members of the press.

It was a quiet vigil, but impressive. The demonstrators stood in a ring around the base of Yui Hill and chanted sutras for the dead. It was an eerie chant, and Randy could tell that the construction workers didn't like it. They kept glancing at the demonstrators as they went about their business.

Promptly at sunset, candles were lit, and at the same time, one of Sawa Industries's homegoing workers turned on his pickup's halogen lights. A candle against halogens, Randy thought and then suddenly the entire thrust of her article leapt into her mind.

She knew exactly how to write it now. She'd start with the description of a lone candle flickering in the twilight, then go on to quote the Japanese proverb about a man being nothing save a candle in the wind. Then she would describe this vigil.

"Minako-san!"

Shin's agitated cry broke into Randy's train of thought. Turning, she saw that Minny was lying on the ground and that Shin was kneeling beside her.

"She fainted," Shin was gabbling. "She just collapsed." He grabbed the prostrate Minny by the shoulders and practically shouted, "Minako-san, *shikari-shite!*—get a hold of yourself!"

Randy asked a group of sympathetic onlookers to step back, knelt down beside Shin and loosened Minako's shirt and belt. Then, as her friend's eyelids quivered open, she said sternly, "You fainted. Now, are you going to listen to reason and go home?"

"I will take you myself," Shin vowed. He looked paler than Minako, and his eyes behind the glasses had a wild look. "I should never have allowed you to come today."

Minny managed to frown. "You forget I am a modern woman," she croaked. "No one tells me what to do. Besides, you needn't trouble yourself, Shin-san. I can go home by myself."

"You cannot walk alone, let alone ride several subway cars. I won't permit it—" Shin rumpled his hair agitatedly as he pleaded, "I mean to say, *please* allow me to accompany you home, Minako-san."

"But our vigil at the rock— We can't both leave," Minako objected.

Randy felt it was time to intervene. She would gladly stand vigil at Yoshitsune's Rock, she said. "It'll help me write my article. Honestly, Minny, I'm glad to do it. Just let Shin-san take you home."

Shin looked so distraught as he guided Minny away that Randy wanted to shout *"Shikari-shite!"* after him. Instead, she went to inform the others of the change in plans.

She half expected the security detail to stop her, but no one interfered when she took a candle and began to walk up the hill. As Randy walked, the chant for the dead rose behind her, and her article began to write itself again.

"Tomorrow a piece of history passes into dust," she murmured. "Tonight vigil candles have been lit. For Junjiro Sawa, head of Sawa Industries, the destruction of Yui Hill is a necessary step. For the Historical Environmentalists gathered here, it means irretrievable loss—"

Her candle's feeble glow gave the scenery an eerie look, and the slope of the hill seemed steeper. "Oh, drat," Randy muttered as she stumbled over a root.

As she fought to keep her balance, memories stirred. The last time she'd been on this hill she had stumbled, too, and Ken had kept her from falling. Even now she could feel his hand clasped about her arm, and the cool night breeze seemed to carry his scent.

Randy realized that she was holding her breath and exhaled forcefully as, concentrating on the roots and stones along the path, she continued to climb. She was aware of the night sounds made by small animals in the underbrush and the sighing of the bamboo in the glade around Yoshitsune's Rock.

It was very dark, and perhaps it was a trick of candlelight that made the rock look bigger, more imposing. Randy put her candle down near the rock, set down her shoulder bag and reached for her tape recorder. She needed to record her impressions of this place.

Clicking on her tape recorder, she began to speak into it. "The feelings that one gets while sitting here in the dark are indescribable," she began. "I don't mean that there's anything frightening or menacing, but I feel a sense of history. Timelessness, maybe. And in spite of the night sounds, there's a hush around Yoshitsune's Rock. An expectant, *waiting* kind of hush—"

There was a rustle nearby, and she tensed. "Who's there?" she demanded.

For answer, there was a muffled curse. "Damned roots are everywhere," Ken's voice replied. "I nearly broke my neck on one."

Had he come to force her to leave her post by the rock? But before Randy could challenge him on that, he growled, "Our security people told me that Naka and his sidekick were holding vigil by the rock. Where are they?"

"Minny got sick and Shin took her home. I'm standing in for them." Randy searched his shadowed face. "Have you come to order me down?"

"Would it do any good?"

"Not likely."

She wished she felt as cool as her voice. Ken had come to stand beside her, and he was so large and powerfully male that his presence made the small clearing seem even smaller. The pale glow of the candle caught the hard lines of his face and delineated the strength of his powerful form. Given all that had happened at their last meeting, Randy had to struggle to keep her composure.

"If I carry you screaming from the hill, your friends will have all the publicity they want," he said abruptly. "That's not why I'm here."

He'd climbed this tiresome hill in order to ensure order, but standing so close to Randy brought too many memories. Her head was tipped back, and though Ken couldn't see her features well, he knew that while her green eyes might be stormy, her lips would be soft. Before his rambling thoughts could continue along this line, he added, "I've decided to keep vigil with you until you decide you've had enough."

"But why?"

"Your friend Naka is a fanatic on the subject of Yoshitsune, and fanatics are capable of ritual suicide," Ken replied. "If he commits seppuku—hara-kiri as Americans call it—on Yui Hill, there'd be more problems and a police investigation. Sawa Town would be considered unlucky, and the big investors would pull out."

"That's nonsense," Randy protested. "Shin isn't even here. Besides, he wouldn't do anything so stupid."

"Oh, no? You don't know these tradition-bound Japanese. Seppuku is the honorable thing to do. It's one of those 'ancient traditions' that you like so much."

The disgust in his voice goaded her to retort, "You seem to care more about Sawa Town than about a man's life. Does building the place mean so much to you?''

It seemed that he hesitated a moment before nodding. "To my father, it means everything."

Randy was puzzled by the odd note in Ken's voice. "How so, when your father already has many triumphs?"

"It's the dream of a lifetime. Do you understand about dreams, Randy?" Again, there was an unreadable note in his deep voice. "Let's agree on an armistice for tonight at least. For different reasons, we're committed to stay on this hill." He paused. "Peace?"

She hesitated only a moment before nodding. "Peace," she agreed. But as she spoke, the glade was suddenly flooded with light.

It was as though a supernova had occurred in the sky. The shadows that had been so thick and dark a moment ago were now limned in silver. "Moonrise," Ken said. "Look."

Randy saw a huge silver globe rise over the tops of the bamboo. "Oh," she breathed. "How incredible!"

But she wasn't looking at the rock or at the glade. She was seeing the way moonlight transformed Ken's face. It silvered his hair and eyes and picked out the hard bones of his face and his strong jaw. He looked as though he were made of light.

"It's a full moon." Ken spoke with difficulty. He'd known Randy was beautiful, but she'd never looked lovelier than now. A familiar ache pulsed in his chest, and it took all his willpower to speak as if nothing were wrong. "Your friends picked a fine night for their vigil, anyway," he commented.

With an effort Randy took her eyes away from Ken and focused on the rock. "Shin said that it was a full moon when *they* met here for the last time."

"That's just a legend, Randy."

He'd spoken sharply, but she persisted. "Maybe, but I can almost *see* it happening. Look, Ken. They must have stood here by the rock when they said goodbye. They loved each other so much, and they were both brave and noble. It must have broken their hearts to know they'd never see each other again."

A small breeze ruffled the bamboo. To Randy, standing in that moon-drenched glade, the sound made by the sharp bamboo leaves mimicked human sighs. The feelings she'd sensed earlier, the quality of *waiting,* intensified.

"Do you feel it?" Randy whispered.

Ken started to ask her what she was talking about. And then he felt it, too. Sorrow, deep and endless, and as dark as the night. Pain that had no beginning and no end. And above all, loneliness. A loneliness that was beyond description and that filled all the perimeters of his mind.

The loneliness reminded Ken of how he had felt when Nora had been killed, but it dug deeper, was stronger and more invasive than that. Ken felt as though he could weep for a hundred years and never be free of this pain.

"What *is* it?" he managed to ask.

Randy couldn't move. All she could do was look at Ken with a helpless, lost look. That look cut the grief and pain that was throbbing through him, and he strode across the few feet that separated them and put his arms around her. He could feel her shiver within their protective circle, and he rested his cheek against her shining hair.

"It's all right, love," he whispered. "I'm here."

And suddenly Randy knew that it *was* all right. The loneliness and pulsing sorrow that had almost paralyzed her ebbed away, and in its stead came a warmth and understanding that gradually built up into an incredible sense of peace and joy. Now Randy felt herself surrounded by a happiness that promised that there would never again be sorrow or pain.

Then that emotion, too, died away. The bamboo stirred in the night wind. A night bird called. The night was just another lovely, moonlit night.

Randy burrowed her cheek against the rough fabric of Ken's jacket and whispered, "What *was* that?"

His voice was subdued. "I don't know."

"Was it like that for *them*, do you think? Is that— is that what we felt?"

Ken's common sense was reasserting itself. "I think what we've got here is a double case of overactive imagination. All that talk about Yoshitsune, and then the moonrise. Let's face it, Randy. Both Yoshitsune and his sweetheart have been dust for hundreds of years."

"I know."

"I don't believe in ghosts."

Randy didn't, either. Or at least she didn't think so.

"What you need is a drink." Ken ran his hand lightly up her arms. "Better yet, a hot toddy. You're trembling."

But she wasn't shivering from cold or from fear. She was reacting to Ken's nearness. As he rubbed his hands up and down her arms, Randy felt her skin begin to tingle. Her heart was pounding like a mad thing. If she didn't put distance between them, right *now*—

She tried to pull free.

"Don't," he said.

Just that, and her heart seemed to stand still. Not just her heart, but the world, the universe itself. In that silent, still place, no one existed but Ken and Randy. No one mattered. All sense and thought fled from Randy's mind as she lifted her face for his kiss.

Their lips met with almost elemental force. It was as though negative and positive fields had found each other. Once more Randy felt an echo of the joy she'd sensed a moment before, but then all thought disappeared. Ken's arms, the passionate mouth that drank from hers, the breath they shared, their hearts, which drummed to the same heady music—these were the only real things in her world.

This wasn't just a kiss, Ken thought dazedly. It wasn't merely the touch of lips, the press of bodies. As he caressed the silky line of Randy's back, as his fingertips mapped the familiar, beautiful curves of her body, he knew the emotion he felt wasn't important just as a prelude to making love. He wanted to love Randy in every way he could, and this physical touching was the best way he knew of being close to her.

He opened his mouth to tell her this, but the words that came were not the ones he'd meant to say. "Randy," he said, "my father's dying."

It was out. The words had been said. Ken waited for guilt to flood through him, but instead of guilt at having broken his promise of silence, he felt an incredible feeling of relief. Then, like water that had been dammed too long, other words came.

As Randy stood in Ken's arms and listened, she wondered why she hadn't guessed what was happening long before this. Perhaps if her tangled feelings for Ken hadn't blunted her reasoning processes, she'd have realized before that Junjiro Sawa was a very sick man. Now she knew that Ken's father had incurable cancer, and that he didn't know it. She understood why Ken had to build Sawa Town before his father died.

Finally Ken's deep voice ebbed into silence and became a part of the greater silence of the glade. Wordlessly Randy held Ken closer. Now she could understand Ken's determination to build Sawa Town and his constant preoccupation with time. Junjiro Sawa didn't *have* much time.

"I'm sorry," she whispered. "Ken, I'm so sorry. But shouldn't your father be told?"

"It's not the Japanese way. Don't get me wrong, Randy, I wanted to tell him, still want to, but the family made a decision and I have to abide by it." Ken rested his cheek against Randy's hair and rocked her lightly back and forth in his arms. "So, now you know."

"I wish you'd told me before this. I wish I could have helped somehow. Ken, it must have been so horrible for you."

"I wanted to tell you, but I'd given my promise to keep silent." She felt his big body quiver with a sigh as he added, "I've broken that vow tonight because I didn't want you to go on believing a lie."

There was a moment's silence. Then Randy spoke in a deeply troubled voice. "You know that I'll never reveal your secret. You *know* that. I'll rewrite my article. But Ken, after what we experienced tonight, how can you bear to destroy this hill?"

"It was our imagination, Randy, it had to be."

"I don't think so." Randy leaned back in the circle of Ken's arms and looked searchingly at him. "But even if we just imagined it, this hill is important to many people. Surely, if you tell your father about them, he'd realize that he can't destroy Yui Hill."

"He's too weak for a confrontation." Ken dropped his arms and turned unhappily away from her. "I haven't got a choice, Randy."

And he didn't. From Ken's point of view, his father's happiness outweighed every other consideration. Ken didn't want Yui Hill destroyed and, left alone, would have gladly taken another path. But against the bonds of duty to his family, he was powerless.

"I guess it's the same old problem," she said sorrowfully. "*Giri* and *ninjo.*"

He turned quickly to face her. "Whatever else we may have imagined, this much is true. Randy, I'm in love with you. Will you at least try and see it my way?''

Randy did try. She did her level best to see Yui Hill through Ken's eyes. The moss was negligible and did no good to anyone. As for Yoshitsune's Rock, it was just a bit of stone. The hill, the rock, the moss— None of these mattered in the large scheme of things.

Then she thought of Minako and Shin. She thought of that moment of despair and glory in the moonlight. "Oh, Ken," she whispered, "I wish I could."

She and Ken were too different. They saw the same truth from opposite points of view. Because he loved his father, Ken was willing to destroy other people's dreams, whereas not for anything, not even for Ken, could Randy have knowingly destroyed someone else's happiness.

Ken read her thoughts in her eyes. Almost convulsively he reached out for her and gathered her into his arms. Then he was kissing her with fierce intensity.

"Randy," she heard him whisper against her lips, "Stay with me tonight. Be with me. We'll work something out—"

His voice was rough with need for her, and his touch was urgent. When he lowered his lips to the V of her shirt, his mouth seemed to singe her skin. "Stay with me tonight," he repeated. "Let me love you."

Nothing in life did she want more than to do just that. She wanted Ken. She loved him. But she also knew that if she stayed with him, the parting would only be harder.

Because go she must, and soon. Since she couldn't bear the thought of watching the hill destroyed, she'd leave tomorrow. The decision stiffened Randy's spine until she felt him stroking her hair.

Never to feel Ken's touch again, never to feel his kiss— Her heart ached. Now I understand how you felt, she thought in the silvered darkness.

With an effort that was more agonizing than physical pain, she pushed Ken gently away.

The light pressure of her hands on his chest said it all. No words were necessary. It was like tearing out his heart, but Ken let her go.

They stood silently for a moment, just looking at each other. Then Randy said, "Goodbye, Ken. Good luck. I don't agree with what you're doing, but—but I wish you all the best."

She picked up her hurricane lamp and walked slowly away from him down the path. He knew that everything they could say to each other had been said and that it was best to end it now, to cut it clean. He also knew that he must forget Randy forever and irrevocably. He needed all his faculties and energies to concentrate on the task before him.

Even so, it took all of Ken's discipline to let Randy walk down the hill and out of his life.

Chapter Ten

The mug at her elbow contained Japanese tea. Randy reached for it and sipped the steaming liquid as she reviewed what she'd written.

"Kien Van Danh is an artist," she read aloud. "In his Spartan apartment, decorated with poems written in beautiful calligraphy—"

Ah, my long lost love.

Randy blinked. For a moment she'd thought she'd heard Ken's deep voice behind her. The impression was so strong that she actually turned her head to look.

Randy shook her head, hard, to clear it. Maybe she'd been working too hard.

She had been back in New York for six weeks. During that time she'd convinced Hal Breeland that the original slant for her article hadn't worked out and had sold him on a new, revised version that barely touched on the Sawas or Sawa Town. She'd had long, heartwarming phone calls with her folks and her siblings and their spouses; she'd had lunch with good friends and a dinner date with a pleasant man; she'd reentered the real world, for crying out loud. So why did she keep getting flashbacks from another time and place?

She thought she'd closed the file on the Sawas four weeks ago when she'd faxed a copy of her revised story to Ken. She'd wanted him to see that she'd kept her promise not to mention anything that might hurt Junjiro. Randy hadn't expected a reply, and she didn't get one. She wasn't the only one who had to get on with life.

Randy took another swig of her tea and focused on the word processor and her current assignment for *Issues Today*. Kien Van Danh had been a refugee, a boat person, who'd arrived in New York ten years ago, penniless and friendless. Danh was also an artist who had made a small fortune in fashion. These days, garments decorated with his delicate art and calligraphy were much in demand. This rags-to-riches story was remarkable in itself, but even more interesting was the fact that Danh had channeled most of his profits into scholarships to help poor youngsters.

It was an angle that appealed to Randy, and she liked Danh, too. He was an unimposing, gentle man who had made her welcome in his modest apartment, offered her a dish of noodles his pretty wife had cooked. They hadn't tasted anything like Dai-suké's noodles, of course, but they'd been good.

If you come with me, I'll show you Happiness.

Randy yelped as she slopped tea all over her shirt and jeans. She got up, found a towel to dry her clothes, then realized that she was too restless to get back to work right away. Instead, she went downstairs to collect her mail. Together with a fat letter from her mother and a number of bills and junk mail, there was a slim envelope fashioned out of blue rice paper.

Minny hadn't written for weeks, so Randy opened this letter first. "Aha!" she cried.

For Minako had written, "This Christmas cake is no more. This September, I am becoming Mrs. Shin Naka. Are you surprised?"

Actually Randy wasn't surprised at all. Grinning with pleasure, she continued to read as Minny explained that this was not at all the match she would have envisioned for herself.

"We are different," Minny had written. "I am loud and noisy. When I am mad, I growl and shout. Shin-san is quiet and meditative. Moreover, I intend to continue with my work at Ohashi University even after marriage. Shin-san is not really pleased, but he agrees I must do as I like." Randy could almost see her small friend's face crinkle with triumph as she continued, "Shin-san is ready to make the compromise! Therefore I am thinking that in spite of the differences, we will be happy together."

Randy thought so, too. Minako now explained that her parents, after nearly expiring from shock, had met Shin's parents. Marriage gifts had been exchanged. "It is official. Will you come to my wedding, Randy? Shin-san and I want you to be with us when we share the marriage sake."

Only family members were permitted to stand before the shrine of the family ancestors and watch the ritual drinking of wine, so Minny's invitation was a great honor. Randy wanted to pick up the phone and call her friend at once, but something held her back from accepting the invitation.

If she went back to Japan, *he* would be there—

Carefully Randy replaced Minny's letter in its envelope and carried her mail upstairs. As she came through the door, the phone began to ring.

"Are you watching TV?" Hal Breeland wanted to know.

"At this time of day? I'm working, for crying out loud."

"Go turn on CBS." Hal sounded excited. "I'll hold."

Randy switched on her set and, with the phone receiver tucked under her ear, turned to sit down. When she faced the TV again, she blinked. Asatsuki was filling the screen of her set.

And there was Yui Hill—at least, a transformed version of the place. Far from being reduced to rubble, the hill stood proudly overlooking a scene busy with construction.

"I don't believe it," Randy gasped.

She turned up the volume on her set and heard the reporter explain that Yui Hill was being transformed into a park. A botanical garden would one day surround Yoshitsune's Rock, and a waterfall, set among Japanese pines, was scheduled to cascade down from its crest.

"This park was designed personally by master-architect Junjiro Sawa," the reporter said, and the cameras now came in for a close-up of Junjiro, who looked pale but very much alive. He spoke in Japanese, and the TV reporter translated. Junjiro had apparently decided to alter his original plans for Sawa Town because he'd learned about the importance of Yoshitsune's Rock and a rare moss that only grew on Yui Hill. A true Japanese, Junjiro concluded, had a duty to preserve important traditions.

Randy belatedly realized Hal was speaking to her. "You're going to have to rework your article, Randy," he was saying. "This is too good to waste. Did you hear what he said about traditions?"

Randy didn't answer her editor because just then the camera shifted again and Ken filled the screen. He looked a little thinner than when she'd seen him last, and his eyes were tired. There were hollows at his cheekbones. His deep voice was just as she'd remembered it, though, and as he spoke about Sawa Town, Randy's eyes blurred with tears. She knew that it wasn't Junjiro's doing that Yui Hill had been spared. Ken had saved it because of what they'd both experienced at Yoshitsune's Rock.

He seemed to be looking directly at her, and even when the cameras moved away, Randy continued to stare at the screen. Ken had done it. Somehow he had managed to save the dreams of so many people. And then another thought surfaced. There was now no reason that she couldn't attend Minny's wedding, no reason why she couldn't see Ken again.

Randy told Hal she'd call him back, replaced the receiver and stared at it. The way she felt now, she didn't want to wait until September. She wanted to fly to Japan right away and be with Ken.

A wave of longing filled her. But then caution, the legacy of generations of Muir midwesterners, surfaced. Perhaps there was a reason why Ken hadn't personally called to tell her about Yui Hill. Perhaps his feelings had changed toward her. At least call him first, the voice of caution warned.

Randy glanced at her watch. It was 1:00 a.m., Japan time. In New York terms, that meant she had to get dressed for a follow-up interview with Kien Van Danh. There'd be time enough to phone Ken this evening, she told herself.

It had started to drizzle, so naturally there wasn't a taxi to be found. Randy put up her umbrella and slogged toward the curb where a yellow cab was veering toward her. She waved frantically at it, then watched it stop for a man some distance away.

Growling under her breath, Randy attempted to flag down another cab. The vehicle seemed to positively sneer at her as it drove past.

"Need a ride?" a deep voice inquired.

He *couldn't* be here. She was hallucinating again. Randy felt her spine go rigid as she very slowly turned around.

The eyes that looked down into her face were tawny. The cut of the nose and jaw were proud. And his mouth— Randy didn't stop to wonder *why* Ken was standing there. She walked blindly into his arms.

Ken had thought he'd carried a picture of Randy in his heart these long weeks, but he now realized that the picture hadn't been good enough. Her eyes were greener than they had been in his memory, and she fit into his arms in a way that made him feel complete again.

For a second they clung together, and then both spoke at once. "What are you doing in New York?" Randy cried.

At the same time, Ken said, "I need to tell you—"

They stopped and looked at each other, both smiling with the joy of seeing each other again. "You look as if you're on the move," Ken said. Indicating a car parked by the curb, he added, "Climb in and I'll drive you wherever you have to go."

They were hardly in the car when questions burst out of Randy. "Why didn't you tell me you were coming to New York? I just saw you on TV—on a segment about the *new* Sawa Town and Yui Hill. How did you manage to save it? How is your father?"

He answered her last question first. "He's better. The doctors are too cautious to talk about remission, but that's what we're hoping for."

"Ken, that's wonderful!"

"As for Yui Hill, I got him to see that it would be bad luck to build Sawa Town on the ill will of others. He agreed."

"It couldn't have been that easy," she exclaimed.

Ken's shrug was eloquent. "After you left, I called the family together and announced that I had decided to tell my father what was wrong with him."

"Oh, my Lord. What did they *say?*"

"They said a lot of things, but in the end I convinced them that I was going to go ahead with or without their approval. I was with my father when the doctors showed him results of certain tests. I think," Ken went on thoughtfully, "that the old man always knew what was wrong but wasn't ready to face reality. Anyway, instead of giving up and dying as the family was afraid he might do, he decided to fight his illness."

Randy leaned over and caught Ken's hand in hers. "I'm *so* glad."

"I wanted to phone you, but it has been one hectic time." Ken covered Randy's hand with his as he added, "You know why I got my father to redesign Sawa Town, don't you?"

"Yes," she whispered, "I know."

"In that case, when do I get to meet your parents?"

"My *parents?*"

He looked at her patiently. "In Japan, it's customary for a man to meet his betrothed's parents. I don't know about New York, but aren't the correct forms observed in Kansas?"

"Ken, this is crazy. We're not engaged."

"I knew I'd forgotten something." They'd come to an intersection, and Ken pulled up at the red light. "Will you marry me?"

"*Marry* you?"

She sounded and looked completely bewildered, and he couldn't blame her. He hadn't meant to blurt out a proposal on a traffic-congested road, for God's sake. But now that Randy was here near him, he didn't want to waste another moment.

"I think I've always loved you," he observed, "even though you're as stubborn as a mule."

"Look who's talking! As if you—"

He swept on, "Also, along with being pigheaded obstinate at times, you show an irritating tendency to be right. Still, you have humor and intelligence and you're beautiful. God, you're beautiful."

Horns had begun to honk violently. "The light's changed," Randy pointed out.

Ken didn't budge. "Will you marry me?" he repeated.

She almost shouted "yes," but then she hesitated, Things were happening so quickly that she hadn't time to assimilate the changes. Marriage was a big step, the biggest, and she needed time to *think*. "You'd better move," Randy said, "or someone will crash into us."

"You didn't answer my question yet." Ken lifted her captive hand to his lips. "Randy, when you left Japan, I told myself it was for the best, that we were worlds apart in our thinking. And we were. Perhaps because I couldn't do anything to keep Nora from dying, I've always felt a need to take charge and dominate my world. You, on the other hand, have always tried to understand people and situations."

She no longer heard the bleep of traffic or the aggrieved shouts of angry motorists who were being forced to drive around them. Randy realized that she was holding her breath.

"You've made me examine my motivations—my own heart, if you will," Ken went on, "and I'm grateful. We may not see eye to eye on every issue, love, but together we'll grow and change. Besides, I can't see my life without you."

"Nor I without you," she whispered.

For wasn't she herself incomplete without Ken? Randy drew a deep breath that was tinged with his distinctive scent and felt as though she'd been lost for a very long time. Now she was finally coming home.

The expression in her eyes made Ken's heart tighten. His voice was husky with emotion as he repeated. "Randy, sweet love of my heart, will you marry me?"

"Yes—" But before she could get any further, there was a howl nearby.

"Buddy, will you *move* that thing? This ain't no private parking lot!"

A truck driver, beefy faced and perspiring with indignation, was shaking a fist at them. There was a cacophony of yells and toots and bleeps. Randy also noted that a police cruiser was edging ominously closer.

"We'd better get out of here," she suggested dreamily.

Then she forgot the world as strong arms enfolded her. Their lips met, and joy welled through her like a river, like a waterfall of light.

It was the happiness she'd sensed that night on Yui Hill, but with a subtle difference. Randy knew that for her and Ken there would be no more partings.

*   *   *   *   *

WRITTEN IN THE STARS

Love's in Sight!
THROUGH MY EYES
by Helen R. Myers

Dr. Benedict Collier was the perfect
Virgo—poised, confident, always in
control . . . until an accident left him
temporarily blinded. But nurse Jessica
Holden wasn't about to let Ben languish in
his hospital bed. This was her chance to
make Ben open his eyes to the *love* he'd
resisted for years!

THROUGH MY EYES
by Helen R. Myers . . . coming from
Silhouette Romance this September.
It's WRITTEN IN THE STARS!

 Silhouette Romance ®

Bestselling author **NORA ROBERTS** captures all the romance, adventure, passion and excitement of Silhouette in a special miniseries.

THE
CALHOUN WOMEN

Four charming, beautiful and fiercely independent sisters set out on a search for a missing family heirloom—an emerald necklace—and each finds something even more precious . . . passionate romance.

Look for THE CALHOUN WOMEN miniseries starting in June.

COURTING CATHERINE
in Silhouette Romance #801 (June/$2.50)

A MAN FOR AMANDA
in Silhouette Desire #649 (July/$2.75)

FOR THE LOVE OF LILAH
in Silhouette Special Edition #685 (August/$3.25)

SUZANNA'S SURRENDER
in Silhouette Intimate Moments #397 (September/$3.29)

 *Silhouette Books®*

FOUR UNIQUE SERIES
FOR EVERY WOMAN YOU ARE...

Silhouette Romance®

Tender, delightful, provocative—stories that capture the laughter, the tears, the *joy* of falling in love. Pure romance...straight from the heart!

SILHOUETTE *Desire®*

Go wild with Desire! Passionate, emotional, sensuous stories of fiery romance. With heroines you'll like and heroes you'll *love*, Silhouette Desire never fails to deliver.

Silhouette Special Edition®

Stories of love and life, these powerful novels are tales that you can identify with—romances with "something special" added in! Silhouette Special Edition is entertainment for the heart.

SILHOUETTE·INTIMATE·MOMENTS®

Enter a world where passions run hot and excitement is the rule. Dramatic, larger-than-life and always compelling—Silhouette Intimate Moments will never let you down.

SGENERIC

SILHOUETTE·INTIMATE·MOMENTS®

IT'S TIME TO MEET
THE MARSHALLS!

In 1986, bestselling author Kristin James wrote A VERY SPECIAL FAVOR for the Silhouette Intimate Moments line. Hero Adam Marshall quickly became a reader favorite, and ever since then, readers have been asking for the stories of his two brothers, Tag and James. At last your prayers have been answered!

In August, look for THE LETTER OF THE LAW (IM #393), James Marshall's story. If you missed youngest brother Tag's story, SALT OF THE EARTH (IM #385), you can order it by following the directions below. And, as our very special favor to you, we'll be reprinting A VERY SPECIAL FAVOR this September. Look for it in special displays wherever you buy books.

Available now at your favorite retail outlet, or order your copy by sending your name, address, zip or postal code, along with a check or money order for $3.25 (please do not send cash), plus 75¢ postage and handling ($1.00 in Canada), payable to Silhouette Reader Service to:

In the U.S.
3010 Walden Ave.
P.O. Box 1396
Buffalo, NY 14269-1396

In Canada
P.O. Box 609
Fort Erie, Ontario
L2A 5X3

Please specify book title with your order.
Canadian residents add applicable federal and provincial taxes.

MARSH-3

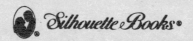 Silhouette Books®

Silhouette Special Edition

presents

SONNY'S GIRLS

by Emilie Richards, Celeste Hamilton and Erica Spindler

They had been Sonny's girls, irresistibly drawn to the charismatic high school football hero. Ten years later, none could forget the night that changed their lives forever.

In July—
ALL THOSE YEARS AGO by Emilie Richards (SSE #684)
Meredith Robbins had left town in shame. Could she ever banish the past and reach for love again?

In August—
DON'T LOOK BACK by Celeste Hamilton (SSE #690)
Cyndi Saint was Sonny's steady. Ten years later, she remembered only his hurtful parting words....

In September—
LONGER THAN... by Erica Spindler (SSE #696)
Bubbly Jennifer Joyce was everybody's friend. But nobody knew the secret longings she felt for bad boy Ryder Hayes....

EVAN
Diana Palmer

Diana Palmer's bestselling LONG, TALL TEXANS series
continues with EVAN....

Anna Cochran is nineteen, blond and beautiful—and she wants
Evan Tremayne. Her avid pursuit of the stubborn, powerfully
built rancher had been a source of amusement in Jacobsville,
Texas, for years. But no more. Because Evan Tremayne is about
to turn the tables...and pursue her!

Don't miss EVAN by Diana Palmer, the eighth book in her
LONG, TALL TEXANS series. Coming in September...only
from Silhouette Romance.